CRAZY
beautiful

JESSICA
SERRA HUIZENGA

Kinsley Moore and Lucas Graham make great friends.
They make even better friends with benefits . . .

Kinsley Moore doesn't believe in love. As an independent, self-determined entrepreneur, she has other things to worry about. Besides, she knows guys are incapable of commitment, so there's no use getting close.

But when she meets Lucas Graham, her new landlord's flirty, sexy son, she's more than up for some casual fun.

Lucas is in no way looking for a relationship either, so when he's offered a no-strings, strictly friends-with-benefits hookup with a beautiful girl, the opportunity is too good to pass up. He's not able to give his heart away, so it's perfect Kinsley prefers to keep emotions out of their arrangement.

Except when Lucas and Kinsley start to feel something more, their complicated pasts threaten to overshadow any chance they might have at a future together.

Can Lucas prove he's capable of love?
Can Kinsley believe she is enough?
This book is for readers over the age of 18 due to strong language and explicit sexual content

For Clifford Peter.
Thanks for putting up with my crazy. xx

CHAPTER

one

Kinsley

"IF YOU COULD JUST SIGN here, here, here, and here, and initial each page, the cottage will be yours, Ms. Moore."

I look up from the stack of documents in front of me and glance to my left at the well-dressed man leaning down beside me. He smells delicious—like cinnamon and soap—and I try not to breathe in too deeply as he points out the places he's referring to on the papers. I shift my eyes to my soon-to-be landlord sitting across the large wooden table. He has silver hair and is wearing a dark blue sweater. He has the kindest eyes I've ever seen. Though younger, he reminds me of my grandfather who used to let me sit on his lap while he solved the daily crossword puzzle in the newspaper. Sometimes he even let me scribble the letters in the boxes. It was simple, but it made me feel special. He died when I was six, so I don't remember much of him, but this man sitting across from me has the same gentle look.

I take a deep breath, grab the pen off the table, and sign and initial my name in all the spots indicated. Then Ryan Blake, the yummy-smelling lawyer, slides the stack of papers across the table so the sweet looking man can scrawl his own signature across the pages.

Kelley Brooks, my realtor slash best friend, nudges my right side from her seat next to me. I know her well enough to know that 1. This is her silent way of congratulating me and 2. Her way of saying, "If you aren't going to pounce on the man standing next to you, maybe I will."

I give her a sideways glance, saying without so many words that she can have him. She knows I'm not interested in a relationship, so if she thinks he has the potential to be Mr. Right, he's all hers. He's cute and all, but I have other things to focus on right now.

"Well, Ms. Moore, I guess that about settles it." The silver-haired man leans forward to hand me a shiny new key. "I am so happy that I get to call such a beautiful, intelligent young lady my new tenant," he says with a genuine grin.

I hold my hand out as he gently places the key ring in my palm, smiling back. "I can't thank you enough Mr. Graham. I'm so excited for this."

"I can tell you are one smart cookie who will do great things. I'm happy to be some small part of your story, so anything I can do to help, you just say the word. And please, call me Eli."

I can't help but smile back real big. I don't know why this man makes me feel so safe. It's odd because I usually don't trust anyone, even if I've known them for a while. It must just be the excitement over my new digs.

I'm so overwhelmed by the fact that I not only just signed a lease to rent my own house, but it's also a big enough place to have more room for my growing floral design business, *Petal*. It's not huge, but compared to my current studio apartment across town the new cottage seems like a palace. The downstairs has a big back room, complete with an adjoining kitchen that will be perfect for my work area. There is also a small office, bathroom, a sitting area in the front, and a loft big enough for a bed and small dresser. Since I started floral arranging two years ago, it's become my dream to someday have my own flower shop. This is one step closer. Now instead of having to fill my bathtub, sink, kitchen table, *and* nightstand with assorted vases, stems, shears, and ribbons, I will have an entire room to work in. Somebody pinch me!

"Ouch!"

Apparently Kelley can read minds, as she just pinched my arm from under the table.

"I'm sure Kinsley here will make us all very proud!" she says. "Our girl has a lot of plans in that big brain of hers, and I know she will do even more amazing things now that she has a bigger place."

I say a silent *thank you* to her for jumping in as I realize I'm still holding out my hand with the key. I snatch it back before thanking Eli again.

"Well, Kinsley, I wish you the best of luck, and please don't hesitate to call me if you have any problems. It's been empty for quite some time, so if anything needs fixing at that place, I will personally make sure it is taken care of for you."

Eli stands up and extends his hand toward me, and thank goodness my mouth finally catches up with my brain. "I certainly will Mr. Grah—Eli," I say as I reach out to shake his hand. I then turn to Ryan to thank him as well. Kelley gets up and follows suit, and I don't miss how her hand lingers in Ryan's for a beat longer than necessary. I swear I even hear her inhale deeply.

I gather up my papers and tuck my new key safely in my

pocket. As Kelley and I head out, she grabs me by the arm and leans over. "Well, you did it, babe. You took the big scary leap and finally signed this lease. I'm so proud I could cry." She pretends to get choked up as we make the short walk out to her car.

To most people, signing a twelve month lease might not seem like a big deal, but considering I never lived anywhere that required more than a month to month agreement, for me this is huge. I don't like being tied down, but something about doing this feels right. This is the first time in five years that I feel like I've regained control over my life.

I look over and nudge her arm. "We both know I couldn't have done it without you. I mean it, Kell. Without your help, I never would have been able to get this place. You are a kick-ass realtor. Not to mention you make a pretty cool best friend, too."

She pretends it's no big deal, but I can see her blush at the compliments. "Don't even mention it. Getting to smell that delicious lawyer was more than worth it. Gosh, I love cinnamon."

"And soap."

"I knew you smelled him, too!" she says with a laugh as we make our way outside. It's a beautiful, sunny New England day. A cool and crisp breeze flows through the trees, making their leaves dance. I sense this will be a new beginning for me as Kelley and I slide into her car and drive off toward East Sweet Street to my new home.

A SHORT RIDE LATER, KELLEY turns her red Honda CR-V left onto East Sweet Street and pulls up the dirt driveway to the cutest house I've ever seen. OK, I may be a little biased since it's now mine, but I swear I thought it was adorable the first time I saw it.

What drew me to this place is the sense of escape. Set back a slight ways from the main road, the white building is sheltered by tons of trees and a wooded area that provides plenty of privacy. Large stepping stones lead toward a small stream off to the left, the bank of which is dotted with wildflowers. On the right side is a beautiful climbing rose bush, the vines entwined across a withered wooden trellis. It has a gabled roof and ornate attic window at the top center. There is a small porch off the front steps and a beautiful forest green door set behind a screen. As Kelley noted the first time we stepped inside, it feels like this place comes straight out of a magical storybook. Now it's my own personal sanctuary.

As I step up onto the porch, I try to remember to take it all in.

This is it, no turning back.

I grab the key from my jacket pocket and insert it into the lock. I step inside and practically squeal out loud. All I've worked for has come down to this moment and I feel so incredibly happy I could burst.

And then, as almost always, my happiness is replaced in a heartbeat with a sudden sadness. An emptiness.

Kelley picks up on it and puts her arm around me. "They're so proud of you, Kins. I know things got all messed up, but you're still allowed to wish your parents could be here to see all your dreams come true in person. Here you are, making shit happen all on your own, just like you always said you would."

I give her a nudge as if to say *I know, but thanks for being the one to say it out loud.* I take a breath and try to gather up as much enthusiasm as I can before saying, "This is going to be great. Thanks again for coming and helping me. I'm glad you're here."

She smiles but stays quiet for a second, and I can tell she wants to say something else. I know what's coming but pretend not to, choosing instead to move up the stairs to the loft attic that will be my bedroom.

Kelley follows and looks around, clearing her throat. "I know I'm great and all, but you also deserve to have someone special to share this with. You know, now that you've committed to a job and a home, maybe you'll consider committing to some . . . other things." She tosses it out all nonchalant but I know what she's getting at.

"Nice try, Kell. Just because I am now a supposed 'responsible' adult with a business and a house doesn't mean I'm ready for a relationship."

She acts like she doesn't know what I'm talking about. "I meant maybe get a dog or something. You know, someone to keep you company." I only have to roll my eyes in her general direction for her to back down. She throws her arms up in mock surrender. "OK, I get it. You're fine by yourself. As usual. I just think you could put yourself out there a little more. You know, maybe date a little."

I cross my arms defensively. "Hey, I date."

"Hooking up with a guy you meet in a bar is not dating." She gives me her stern *you know I'm right* look.

"That happened once!" I shoot back indignantly. She raises her eyebrow, causing me to relent. "OK, twice. But the second time doesn't count because I only made out with him a little before he passed out."

Kelley just laughs and shakes her head.

The funny part is I don't even drink. Getting tipsy might mean losing control of a situation, and I refuse to let that happen. Not since every man I thought I could trust turned out to be a liar. I've learned to keep my guard up.

Sure, I might not always make the best decisions when it comes to guys, but at least I know what I'm getting myself into. It's not a crime to have casual sex if we're both consenting adults.

The few times Kelley has convinced me to go out, we make quite the pair: I stay sober and end up having meaningless sex while she gets completely drunk but will barely even kiss a guy if she doesn't see the potential for a lasting relationship.

"Besides, you're not exactly tied down either," I remind her. "If you keep holding out for Prince Charming you might be waiting forever." I've known Kelley since we were seven and used to reenact fairy tales with our Barbies. We may have both grown out of playing with dolls, but I think Kelley still believes Ken & Barbie are soul mates and everything always has a happy ending. Ever the romantic, she's only had one serious relationship with her high school sweetheart. When that ended she decided not to waste her time on anyone who might not be "the one."

Kelley turns and sits down on the top step leading up to the loft. "True, but there's one difference between you and me, Kins." She looks back at me. "I am at least open to having a relationship. If you really don't want one then that's your call, but you're so closed off I'm afraid you might miss out on a chance at something—or someone—really great."

I sit next to her on the stairs and pat her knee playfully in an attempt to lighten the mood. I know she means well but I don't want to think about letting anyone else into my life. I have enough going on with my business and my new place. "I'm good with the way things are, but how about this—I promise if I ever bump into Prince Charming, I'll give him your number instead, OK?"

She shakes her head but smiles. "OK, deal." She knows I'm stubborn and won't change my mind, so thankfully she drops it. She gets up to head back downstairs. As she makes her way to the front door she calls back, "If I can't get you to settle down, at least I can help you settle in. Come help me with the boxes and we can get this show on the road."

I wait a minute before following her. If I'm being honest with myself, part of me does kind of wish I didn't have to be on my own *all* the time. I'd never admit it out loud, but lately I've been feeling a little emptier than usual. Despite things looking up with *Petal* and my new living situation, there still seems to be something missing. I keep such a tight hold on my emotions that it can be exhausting. If only I could just let go . . .

I take a deep breath and steel myself. *No, this is what you wanted. What you worked for. Independence. Self-reliance. Control. It's just you against the world, and you're going to protect yourself by keeping everyone else out of it. Stick to casual hookups if you're lonely and you won't get hurt.*

CHAPTER

two

Kinsley

THE NEXT WEEK FLIES BY in a blur of petals and paint. Not only have I been trying to get myself settled in at the cottage, but I still have a business to run. I spent the first few days here painting walls, emptying boxes, and rearranging furniture, but for the past forty-eight hours I've pretty much been locked away in the workroom, stopping only to grab a quick bite and catch a few hours of sleep.

Tonight I have one of my biggest jobs: an extravagant wedding which includes thirty centerpieces, a bridal bouquet, eight bridesmaid's bouquets, nine boutonnieres, a floral archway for the ceremony, and a basket of petals for the flower girl. Every waking hour has been spent trimming stems, arranging bouquets, and tying ribbons.

At night, while I eat a quick dinner, I have also been answering emails, updating my website, and sourcing supplies needed for the rest of my upcoming orders. I'm a stickler for details, so everything down to the ribbon color and vase shape for each and every arrangement has to be completely perfect. There may be some unexpected things that happen in my life, but my work definitely falls under the category of "Things Kinsley Can Control."

It takes a lot to wear all the different hats required to keep this business running by myself, but I absolutely love that I can be consumed by and passionate about my work. It gives me both freedom and purpose. I've loved flowers ever since I was a little girl and, after a string of random, temporary jobs, I somehow got lucky and landed a position in a florist shop a few years ago. I started as an assistant, sweeping the floors and cleaning out the coolers, but eventually Mary, the owner, let me start designing my own arrangements. She said I was a natural. When she decided to retire and moved to Colorado, she encouraged me to continue designing on my own, which is how *Petal* was born.

While someday I want to have a full florist shop & nursery, right now I'm focusing on floral arrangements for weddings— yes, the irony of which is not lost on me. I'm good at it, and they're the jobs that not only pay the best, but also keep me busiest. It's a great way to start building a professional name for myself. Plus, I'd rather be busy so that I don't have time to focus on what might be lacking in my life. So what if I'm alone? I get my fill of happy couples and sappy love crap with the weddings I work on, so no need to try and experience it myself. I hate to sound like such a cynic when it comes to love, but the truth is I just don't believe it really exists. At least not in any lasting, always-forever-and-a-day kind of way.

Every time I meet with a new bride and she gets all glassy-eyed and emotional when talking about marrying the man of her dreams, I can't help but feel jealous—not because she has someone, but because she actually believes love will last. From my own personal experience, men are incapable of committing themselves to one woman forever, so why go through with the whole charade? It's just the way the world works and I've learned to accept it. I can still find joy in arranging flowers for the big day, even if I think marriages themselves are a dead end.

It's now almost two o'clock, which means I have to get going if I want to have enough time to set up before the ceremony starts at six thirty. I load the last of the flowers into my Honda Pilot and head toward Woodwind Hills, a fancy banquet hall on the other side of town.

When I arrive, the wedding planner directs me where to park and unload, and I spend the next four hours transforming the dining room and patio into a floral wonderland. Since the wedding has a vintage-modern theme, I went with a combination consisting mainly of white roses, light pink peonies, and purple lisianthus. I also added a bit of maidenhair fern and baby's breath for a delicate, whimsical touch.

I step back to examine the archway. Set across four connecting wooden beams, I draped the flowers across the top and down the sides, adding the largest, boldest flowers to the left side, forming an asymmetrical focal point. As the center of the entire ceremony, I want to make sure it looks right. I adjust a few stems and then make my way back inside. I duck into the restroom to splash a little water on my face and attempt to tame my hair. After a few hours of work I'm pretty dirty and sweaty, so I try to make myself look at least a little presentable before delivering the bouquets and congratulating the bride, my last task before heading home. I pile my hair on top of my head and make my way upstairs.

I knock on the door of the bridal suite and am welcomed in by a group of expertly primped and overly perfumed bridesmaids. The air is so thick with hairspray I can barely breathe, but

I keep my composure as I hand out each of the bouquets—to much *oohing* and *ahhing*—and then I am ushered over to the bride who tears up a little when she sees herself in the full length mirror, bouquet in hand, donning a beautiful beaded gown with her hair pinned up, a long lace veil trailing behind.

She really does look happy, and for a moment, I actually have the slightest glimmer of hope for girls like her. As much as I might not believe in true love, that doesn't mean I want to shatter the illusion for my more optimistic clients. Who knows? Maybe one of them ends up truly getting their happily ever after.

Oh lord, I really have been hanging out with Kelley too long . . .

The mother of the bride air hugs me and I tell her that everything looks beautiful before I say my goodbyes to the rest of the party. I make my way back down the stairs where the banquet staff is buzzing around the room, making sure every last detail is set before the ceremony begins. As I pass by the window looking out over the patio, I can see guests are already starting to arrive. With all of the tuxedo-clad men and women wearing dazzling dresses, it looks more like some sort of red carpet event. I gather up the last of my tools and empty boxes when I notice one of the smaller centerpieces on a cocktail table outside has a few wilted stems drooping over the side. I glance down at my dirty jeans and t-shirt, then back out at the gathering crowd. Most of the guests are taking their seats further down the lawn by the archway, so I decide to make a quick dash outside before anybody notices me.

I exit the double doors leading out from the dining room where I walk quickly to the high-top table. I pluck the wilted stems from the gold vase and adjust the remaining flowers. I might think this whole fairy tale thing is ridiculous and just for show, but if I'm going to put my name and reputation on these flowers it's the least I can do to make sure they're perfect. I smooth down the black linen, make sure the vase is centered, and turn to make my way back inside, passing more guests as they make their way out to their seats.

I keep my head down, trying not to draw more attention to the fact I look like such a hot mess, but I catch a quick glimpse of a tall, extremely handsome man walking past with a gorgeous woman by his side. Something about the way he smiles at his girlfriend—or who I assume is his girlfriend—makes me do a double take and look back as they continue down the lawn. They obviously don't notice me, and before I can stop myself, I think it must be nice to have someone look at you like that . . . like you're the reason he's so happy.

I realize I'm holding my breath as I stare at the stranger walking away for a moment longer.

I take a deep breath before shaking my head and turning back toward the doors.

You're probably just reacting to a hot guy with a cute ass, Kins. Get a grip.

Hey, just because I'm not interested in a relationship with a man doesn't mean I can't enjoy admiring one . . .

When I get back inside, I grab the rest of my stuff, load it into the car, and head back home, spending the entire drive trying to shake the image of the man with the captivating smile out of my mind.

CHAPTER

three

Lucas

"I LOOK LIKE A FUCKING penguin. This cummerbund is stupid."

"Aw come on, Luc. I think you look cute."

I go to punch my best friend, Ryan Blake, in the arm, but he ducks out of my reach. *Stupid fucking tux.*

"Who the hell wants a black tie wedding nowadays anyway?" I pull on my sleeves feeling oddly uncomfortable. I'm no stranger to wearing a tuxedo, but for some reason today it's really irritating me.

I hear Ryan shuffle behind me. "Hey, I hear you, man. If I were to ever get married—which, by the way, we both know isn't going to happen—but *if* I was, just give me a beach, a barbecue, and a babe and I'd be good to go."

I fidget with my bow tie, trying to make it feel less restrictive. I feel bad for my buddy Sean, who's marrying his long-time girl, Danielle. If I'm feeling this suffocated in my tux and I'm only a guest, I can only imagine how he's feeling.

Ryan continues, "Look on the bright side—I'm sure there is at least one hot bridesmaid in particular who would be willing to help you out of that later."

I see the reflection of Ryan's smirk in the mirror, knowing damn good and well which bridesmaid he's referring to. We're standing in my bedroom, and I'm trying to prolong going to this thing. We haven't really been close with Sean since we graduated from UMASS six years ago, but we still have mutual friends and his soon-to-be mother-in-law apparently invited anyone either of them ever said two words to. Something about this being the social event of the year or some bullshit. The only reason I agreed to go was to support an old friend.

Well, that, and the fact Ryan thought it would be funny if he put me down as his plus one.

I shoot Ry an unimpressed look as I untie my bowtie yet again and start over. "You know I'm not interested in her like that anymore." I return my focus to the tie, hoping to convey the fact that this conversation is over.

Ryan stays quiet for a minute, jamming his hands in his pockets as he leans back against the wall, silently chewing a piece of gum. I think he's going to drop it, but no such luck. "So are you pissy because you haven't gotten laid in a while, or are you upset because part of you is thinking it could have been you and Chelsea standing up there today?"

I usually appreciate Ryan's directness, but sometimes his straight-to-the-point attitude is a little unnerving . . . as well as eerily on point.

I continue to look in the mirror and adjust the tie one last time. "I haven't gotten laid because it's my choice. You know that, so don't be a dick." Once I finish, I turn to look at him. "And just because Chelsea wanted it, doesn't mean it was right."

Chelsea is a good friend of Danielle's, and as such is one of her bridesmaids. Chelsea and I dated back when we graduated. We were together for five years and things were good. Comfortable. But then she started hinting that she wanted more of a commitment. I sort of let her believe we would get married, but ultimately I didn't see myself settling down. We split, but things ended pretty amicably. It's been two years and we're still friends. She even works for one of my clients. Ryan always warns me that she still thinks we're going to end up together, and OK, maybe I am kind of an asshole for keeping her close. But she was a part of my life for so long that I can't just cut her off. Don't get me wrong, I've made it clear that we're only friends now, but she likes pretending we might still have a chance . . . and I guess I like knowing someone still cares about me. It's fucked up, but it's just how it is with us.

The real truth is that ever since my mom died when I was thirteen, I've never been able to get close to a girl. I watched how horrible it was for my dad to lose the love of his life and I vowed never to allow myself to go through that. When I met Chelsea I thought I could change, but turns out I only liked the company . . . having someone there for me when I needed or wanted it. Eventually it wasn't fair to lead Chelsea on, so I ended it. I told her she deserved someone who can give her every part of him, which is the truth. I'm not that guy, but she thinks maybe someday I can be.

After we broke up, I slept with just about any woman who looked my way, trying to feel something, which obviously wasn't the answer to my problems either. So for the past six months I've been trying to change. I'm not capable of love, but I'm also tired of the random, one-night stands.

Now if only I can find a girl who understands the meaning of casual, things would be perfect.

Ryan moves toward the door. "Hey, you're preaching to the choir, brother. I can tell she's not the one for you. I'm just waiting for you to cut her loose since she still looks at you like she's picturing your white picket fence, golden retriever, and two point five kids. The sooner you shut that shit down for good, the better."

Before I even get two words out, Ryan changes the subject as if nothing happened. "Now, if you're done getting dressed, princess, we have a ball to attend." He gestures to the door and holds out his elbow as if he's really going to escort me. I grab my jacket from the bed and head past him, giving him a light shove on my way through.

He pretends to be offended. "Playing hard to get? Oh, I see. You're not easy on a first date." As I make my way to the door, I hear him call out, "I can respect that, but know I love the chase!"

I crack up and grab my keys. I know I'm lucky to have such a good friend. As much as he likes to bust my balls, Ryan will always look out for me. I can count on him to always have my back, and at least he will help keep me sane tonight.

WE PULL UP TO WOODWIND Hills a short while later. As soon as we make our way out back we are immediately flanked by Tamra and Jennifer, old friends whom we haven't seen since graduation. Tamra, who had a *very* brief fling with Ryan sophomore year, envelops him in a giant hug.

"OMG it's been forever since I've seen you!" Tamra squeals. Ryan looks uncomfortable as she holds on long enough to make it awkward. Finally, she releases him. "You HAVE to come sit next to me so we can catch up."

She pulls him toward the rows of seating lined up further

down the lawn, leaving me alone with Jennifer.

"Sorry about her." Jennifer nods to where Tamra is still pulling a reluctant Ryan. "She's just excited. She thinks this is some sort of reunion." Jenn looks embarrassed for her friend.

"Don't worry about it. Ry's a big boy. He can take care of himself." We look over to see Tamra re-introducing Ryan to a group of former sorority girls, who all start hugging and patting him like he's their new pet. He looks back at us and mouths the word "Help." It takes a lot to rattle Ryan, but this has clearly thrown him off his game. I shrug at him, then grin at Jennifer before saying, "Maybe not," which makes us both laugh.

Jenn and I were always pretty friendly, and are able to fall back into a comfortable conversation as we catch up.

"So, I hear you started some successful venture capital firm?" she asks as we continue walking toward the chairs. I nod and she adds, "What's that like?"

I'm about to answer when a woman over to my left by the cocktail tables catches my attention.

Dressed in a plain t-shirt and jeans with her brown hair pulled on top of her head in a haphazard—yet adorable—way, she seems pretty intent on making sure the flowers in the center of the table are perfect. The way she gently bites her bottom lip and is so completely focused mesmerizes me. Here I am, surrounded by tons of women who are all dolled up and wearing expensive dresses, yet I can't take my eyes off this unassuming one. There's something about her that is completely compelling. I can't help but smile as I try to imagine more about her. What's her name? Does she work here? What's her favorite color?

I hear Jennifer say my name, and I realize I forgot to answer her question.

I continue to smile, directing my gaze at Jenn as an apology for zoning out. "Oh you know, it pays the bills. Plus being my own boss always has its perks."

I try to stay engaged in our conversation, but glance back over to catch another look at the mystery girl. She's no longer at the table. My gaze narrows just in time to see her walk a few steps before disappearing into the building.

Jennifer and I find a pair of seats next to Tamra and Ryan. I shake my head to snap myself out of whatever it was that just happened. Maybe it *has* been too long since I've gotten laid.

As I sit down next to Ryan, he leans over and whispers out of the side of his mouth, "Thanks for helping me out back there, asshole."

I whisper back in my best baby voice, "What's the matter? Did those big, scary girls hurt you?"

He elbows me before glancing around, making sure nobody is watching him. "When does the bar open?"

I chuckle. "Why? You don't drink."

"I know that, dipshit. But the sooner they get wasted," he motions to the group of girls now waving at him, "the sooner I can get the hell out of here alive."

I can't help but crack up as we hear the string quartet strike the first few notes of *Here Comes the Bride*.

CHAPTER

four

Kinsley

IN THE WEEKS FOLLOWING THE Woodwind Hills wedding job I have more time to focus on fixing up the cottage. There have been a few minor issues—a squeaky door here and a stuck window there—but Eli has been extremely responsive and helpful in getting them fixed. The first couple of times I felt bad calling him. I mean, I can repair a window myself, right? How hard could it be? But he had insisted I notify him about any issue whatsoever, so I felt it was my duty as a responsible tenant to let him know.

I also get the sense he gives me a little more attention than a typical landlord would, but we both seem to enjoy the company. We've gotten to chatting a few times, and I find he really is as kind as he seems.

He is mostly retired, except for maintaining the couple investment properties he owns, and he likes to spend his free time fishing and building model airplanes. He loves to listen to Dean Martin, takes his coffee black, and his son calls him every day. I get the impression his wife passed away some time ago, but I've never felt right pressing for more details.

I'm expecting him any minute, as he called this morning to ask if he can stop by to check on the repairs. I hear a knock at the door so I close my laptop and jog to the front to greet him.

"Hey there, Kinsley. Just wanted to check the job those guys did on the window yesterday. It's not giving you anymore trouble now, is it?"

"Hey, come on in. They did a great job and it's perfect now." We step into the front room and I motion toward the kitchen. "I can make some coffee if you'd like."

He waves his hands out in front of him, politely declining. "Oh thanks so much for the offer, but I can't stay long. I'm heading out on an extended vacation—a fishing trip I take every year with an old friend. I'll be gone for a month so I wanted to leave you my son's number. Lucas will be looking after things while I'm gone. I want you to be sure to call him if you need anything at all."

He hands me a scrap of paper with a phone number scribbled across it.

"OK, great. Thanks." I accept the offered slip of paper. "I think things will settle down for me now and I won't need much else for a while." I notice I feel a little sad he's leaving. Not that I'm dependent on him or anything, but there has been something nice about having the regular company of a father-like figure. Once or twice I found myself wondering what it would be like to grow up with a dad like Eli. Would things have turned out differently for me?

But those are things I prefer not to think about, so it's probably best I won't see him for a while.

"I'll be back before you know it and I'm sure you'll be the talk of the town as our newest, most successful business. I hate to leave at such a pivotal time, but the place is looking great and I know you'll be in good hands." He makes his way back to the door, but stops just as he reaches for the handle. "And don't let Lucas fool you. The boy can be a bit of a wise-guy, but I promise he'll take care of you."

The way he says that last part makes my belly do a little somersault. *Get it together, Kinsley. He means he'll take care of the cottage.*

"Hopefully I won't need to bother him, but I can handle a wise-guy, don't you worry."

Eli lets out a small chuckle. "Oh I have no doubt you can handle him. In fact, I'm counting on it." He winks before turning to let himself out.

I close the door behind him just as I hear my cell phone begin to ring. I hurry to the office and stick the scrap of paper with his son's number on my desk before picking up the call.

"Kell, what's up?" I say.

"So you *are* still alive. Good to know. Now I can call off the search party," she quips.

"Yeah . . . sorry. I guess I have been MIA lately. I've just been really busy getting this place up and running."

"I know, Kins, but you gotta come up for air sometime. Running yourself ragged isn't going to do you or your business any good. As your friend, I insist you come with me to this launch party thing on Friday night. My firm helped a new company find their office and they are having some big to-do to celebrate. Rumor is they got some pretty big investors, so it's going to be over the top. Either way, it's free drinks, not to mention the chance to get all dressed up with my best girl, who, by the way, desperately needs to get out more."

"Yeah, sure. That sounds good." I feel bad for being so out of touch lately, and I guess I could use a night of fun. "Pick me up at seven?"

"You got it, babe. See you then."

"SHIT. OUCH. DAMN."

Ugh, why does this have to be so difficult?

It's been two days since Eli stopped by and I'm laying on my back with my head under the sink trying to figure out how in the hell to fix it. It seems to be clogged and I really don't want to have to bother his poor son with my silly problem. But considering I don't have the first clue about what plumbing part does what, I opt to give in.

I push myself up and move across the hall to rifle around on my desk for the piece of paper with Lucas' number on it. I grab my cell phone and dial the digits.

"Hey, you've reached Lucas Graham. I can't get to the phone right now, but leave me a message and I'll get back to you as soon as I can."

The sexiness of this man's deep, rich voice is enough to distract me from why I had to call in the first place. Thankfully the loud *beep* on the other end snaps me out of my trance.

"Hey, Lucas. This is Kinsley Moore. I recently signed the lease for the cottage on East Sweet Street. Your dad said to call you if I had any problems and while it's not a big deal, the sink is clogged. If you could give me a call when you get a chance that would be great. Thanks." I recite my phone number and hang up.

I return to the kitchen and stare at my phone as if he will actually call me right back. Hello, I'm sure he has a life. And a job. Of course he has a job! He probably won't be able to get back to me until tonight, if then. Not sure what else to do, I stick my head back under the sink to take one last peek. It's then I get the brilliant idea to look online for some videos on how to unclog a drain.

And that is when all hell starts to break loose.

The video makes it look so easy—grab a wrench, unscrew the little pipe thingy, and make sure there is nothing stuck in there. Easy peasy, right?

Wrong.

When I grab my wrench and begin to do what the man in the video does, the next thing I know water is shooting out.

Everywhere.

Startled, I try to stop it but drop the wrench in the process. The spray is so bad I can't see where it fell, so I look around for a bucket or something to catch the water. All I see are vases full of arrangements I finished up the day before—it only took me three hours to get them perfect.

Screw it, this is an emergency!

I leap up, grab a handful of flowers to yank them out of their vase, throw them behind my head, and thrust the container at the continuously spraying stream. I do this over and over until six vases are emptied of their contents, yet the water keeps on coming. Desperate and frantic, I grab my phone and dial the most recent number.

"Hey, you've reached Lucas Graham. I can't get to the phone right now, but leave me a message and I'll get back to you as soon as I can."

"Hey, this is Kinsley again. Sorry to call again but the problem with the sink seems to have gotten worse. Water is spraying everywhere and I can't make it stop . . . I'm sure you're at work so I guess I can try to call a plumber. I wanted to let you know since I already left you that other message. OK great thanks bye."

Hang up the phone, idiot.

Ugh. Apparently a high stress situation makes me word vomit all over the place. Poor Lucas. I'm sure he thinks his dad's new tenant is a complete crazy lady. Unfortunately, there's no time to dwell on that right now.

I dive to my knees again and scramble to locate the wrench I dropped. I finally find it and try again to tighten back up whatever I apparently *untightened*. By an act of God, it actually stops.

Soaked and panting I look around to assess the damage: Sopping jeans? Check. Destroyed kitchen? Check. Hours of work and inventory lost? Check.

Fucking YouTube.

After what must be fifteen minutes of just sitting here contemplating what to do next, I stand up and can barely move. My tank top and jeans are so wet they're practically a second skin. Not wanting to drip water any further than it has already gone—and needing the freedom to actually bend my legs—I decide to strip off my pants here. Then I can dart upstairs to change before finding the number for a plumber. I face the sink, my back to the half closed door, and shimmy my way out of the soaked garment. I step out of the soggy bundle of denim and reach down to pick it up.

And that's when I hear it . . . the sexy, deep voice I can't help but recognize.

"Nice stems."

CHAPTER

five

Lucas

BZZ. BZZZZ.

Damn, that's the second call from the same number. I look down at the flashing screen on my vibrating phone, which indicates I have two new messages. I'm sitting in my home office trying to get some work done without any distractions, but this might be important. I pick up the phone and hit the play button to listen to the voicemails.

The first is from a confident-sounding woman named Kinsley. I remember my dad telling me about his new tenant. *"Make sure you take good care of her, Luc. I don't think she has many people around but she's smart and very talented. I can tell she's use to being independent, but she really doesn't know much about fixing up a place. Bless her heart for trying, though. I want to make sure she feels comfortable in the new place—after all you know how special it is to us."*

Yeah, I knew. When he told me he wanted to rent out the cottage I wasn't sure how to feel. We kept it empty on purpose for the past fifteen years, only stopping by occasionally to make sure it was in decent shape. There were always offers to buy or rent, but until this woman, Kinsley Moore, came into the picture, dad never seemed interested. I figured he thought it was time to move on or make some extra cash and I didn't want to ask questions.

Just as the first message ends and I'm thinking about how soft and gentle her voice is and how sexy my name sounds on her lips (*really, dude?*), the second one starts and she is obviously freaked out. While it's difficult to hear over the sound of rushing water, her message basically comes out as one long sentence said in a single breath and I hear lots of noise in the background. She sounds different from her first message—the strong, confident woman replaced with a scared and defeated one. I can tell she's trying to remain calm, but the anxiety in her voice gives her away. I instinctively feel some primal need to rescue her.

The cottage is right around the corner from my apartment and, not wanting to waste time by trying to call back, I jog to the door, grab my keys from the counter and my favorite leather jacket from its hook, and head out to the elevator.

A FEW MINUTES LATER I pull my white BMW Gran Coupe into the dirt drive on East Sweet Street and cut the ignition. I hop out and make my way to the front door. I try knocking, but when she doesn't answer I realize she probably can't hear it. I try the handle, finding it unlocked, so I push my way inside. Finding Kinsley and making sure she is OK is the only thought on my mind. The place is pretty quiet as I head toward the back.

The door to the entryway of the kitchen is half open and I

can already see a bunch of bent and broken flowers littering the floor. I crouch down to pick one up as I push open the door fully with my left hand.

And that is when my breath catches in my fucking throat.

Standing before me is the most beautiful little body I've ever seen. Her back is to me so I can't even see her face, but her smooth, creamy legs are slowly revealed as she sticks her ass out and pushes her soaked pants down them. Her long, wavy brown hair falls around her shoulders and is damp as if she's just gotten out of the shower.

I grip the already battered flower in my right hand and rake my eyes one more time from her heels up her calves and thighs to the perfect curve of her ass covered in a sexy as hell pair of pink lace panties. I try to think of something to say and end up blurting out, "Nice stems."

Smooth, Lucas. Real smooth.

The woman in front of me is just starting to pick up the recently removed piece of clothing when she freezes. *Shit, I've made her uncomfortable, obviously. Nice one, bro. Quick, say something to make this a little less embarrassing.*

"Already soaked for me I see. And to think we only just met."

Douchebag.

It's then that she slowly turns toward me, holds the wet jeans out and shrugs.

"Yeah, except you took so long I had to finish without you."

And as I look up at her and recognize her gorgeous face, with stormy blue eyes and full lips that curve up into a tempting, flirty smile, I know instantly I am in trouble.

Big, big trouble.

CHAPTER

six

Kinsley

AS I GRAB MY PANTS off the floor I know I have a decision to make. I can let my mortification get the best of me and try to disappear right into this very spot, or I can take charge of the situation and laugh it off.

"Yeah, except you took so long I had to finish without you."

Clearly I choose the latter.

As I turn around with as much confidence as I can muster, I draw in a sharp breath. It's him. The guy I noticed at the wedding. Since I haven't been able to get his face out of my mind for the past two weeks, I'd recognize it anywhere.

He's even more gorgeous up close, and the look on his face is a mixture of what seems like amusement and . . . lust? Nah, I'm sure he's just trying not to laugh.

After a beat, he collects himself enough to respond.

"Touché. Kinsley, right? I'm Lucas. I got your messages and

came right over, but it looks like you may have things under control?"

He cocks his eyebrow and looks around as he says that last part.

"Well, I got it off, but I don't think it will last." I, too, glance around and gesture to the mess around me. God, why is everything sounding so dirty right now? I quickly realize I'm also still standing here in a wet tank top without any pants on, and move my hands holding the soaked jeans in front of my crotch.

As if he hasn't already seen too much . . .

At least I'm wearing cute underwear. Silver lining and all that.

He doesn't take his eyes from me as he relaxes against the doorframe. "Since I'm here, is there anything else I can help you with?" If I didn't know better, I'd swear he meant that statement to have an altogether different implication. Considering he hasn't run from the room screaming and shielding his eyes at least boosts my confidence some. Maybe he doesn't mind what he sees?

Or he sees half naked women all the time, and I'm nothing special.

Damn it, confidence deflated.

Suck it up, Kins. If you play this off as no big deal, maybe it won't be one.

"If you don't mind, I'd like to run upstairs and get changed." I wait for him to take that as his cue to leave.

Without taking his eyes off me, he replies with an easy, "Sure, I'll just take a look under the sink while you do that."

I coolly make my way to the door but turn back to warn, "You might want to be careful—it doesn't like to play nice."

"Thanks for the tip. I'll be careful." He flashes another panty dropping grin.

Well, my pants are already off. Might as well really embarrass myself and bare it all.

Thankfully, I pull it together, manage to keep the rest of my clothes on, and force what I hope comes off as an easy-going grin. I quickly shimmy past him and jump across the hall to the stairway.

When I get upstairs, I replace my wet tank top with a sweater and throw on a pair of curve-hugging jeans. I run my fingers through my hair and can only imagine how awful I look. What an awesome way to make a first impression. I can see him telling this story to a bunch of friends as they laugh so hard their stomachs hurt.

I take a deep breath and try to regain some composure before heading back downstairs. When I get to the kitchen, I see Lucas laying on a towel with his head under the sink. Now that I'm fully clothed and have a second to gather my wits, I have the chance to really look at him.

He's tall. Like, really tall. But then again, at only five-two just about anybody seems tall to me. I'd say he's definitely north of six feet, maybe six-two. He's wearing brown boots and the most flattering pair of jeans that are doing all sorts of amazing things for his lower half. He has a on a white t-shirt that hugs him perfectly with a brown and tan flannel button up tied around his waist. He was previously wearing a worn leather jacket, which I now see tossed up on the counter.

As if he can sense me practically undressing him with my eyes, he leans up on his elbow from under the sink, giving me a chance to look at his oh so gorgeous face. Short, messy brown hair, square jaw covered in the sexiest bit of stubble, and the most intense hazel eyes.

"I think I've got this fixed for you, at least for now. I'll call a professional to come and make sure everything else is fine though, just in case." The look of concern in his eyes warms me. I seem to get the same warm feelings around Lucas that I do around his dad. Safety. Comfort. *Damn, those are some good family genes.*

Then again, I feel quite a few other things that are nowhere close to what I feel around his dad.

"Thanks. I really hope I didn't ruin anything." I don't want him to think I don't care for this place.

He chuckles and runs his hand through his hair in an impossibly sexy gesture. "Well, I wouldn't go quitting your day job to become a plumber or anything, but no major harm done. Next time you might want to try shutting the water off before you decide to go messing with pipes though."

I smile back. "Ah . . . right. I guess I forgot that part. My bad." I fidget with my hands. Lucas has got me feeling all sorts of anxious, from my unintended little peep show and our playful, dirty banter, to the intense look he keeps giving me that I can't quite read. I'm usually much more composed, so I'll chalk my anxiety up to the adrenaline boost resulting from the recent excitement.

"No worries," he says. "I'm sorry I didn't pick up your first call. I'm impressed you took matters into your own hands and at least tried to fix it yourself. Most girls I know wouldn't even touch a wrench, let alone try to use one." He shifts his weight to lift himself up from the floor, placing the wrench on top of the counter.

I blush at his compliment. "I like to be able to take care of myself. I hated to have to call and bother you, but I also promised Eli that I would let him know if anything was wrong here. Since he is away and gave me your number, I wanted to let you know about the drain. I realized too late that you were probably at work or something. Speaking of, were you at work? I really don't want to be any trouble."

"I'm glad you called. This place means a lot to my dad . . . and to me. So don't worry about bothering me. And let's just say my boss is pretty cool and won't mind me stepping out for a bit."

"Well, thanks. I appreciate it. And I promise to be more careful. I'll clean this mess up and let you get back to work." I start picking up some of the mutilated flowers strewn across the floor. I start gathering them up when I notice Lucas is doing the same. "You don't have to do that."

He shrugs. "No big deal. It will go a lot faster with the two of us. Plus my dad would kick my ass if he knew I left his new favorite tenant to deal with this all on her own." He winks and I just about choke on my own tongue.

I avert my eyes from his gaze and try to focus on cleaning up. "Your dad?" I ask incredulously. "He doesn't seem like he could hurt a fly."

"He wouldn't hurt a fly. His son, however? He won't hesitate to put me in my place."

"Sounds like you speak from lots of experience," I say with an accusing tilt of my head.

"Unfortunately, yes. I can be quite a handful. My old man is always there to remind me to get my shit together when I fuck up. He'll point out what I did wrong one minute, and help me fix it the next."

The look of pure respect shows plainly on his face. "Sounds like you guys are close."

I think back to hearing Eli mention how he talks to his son every day. Hot *and* loyal? Sweet lord, this man has perfection written all over him. In theory, that is . . . I'm sure he still has a few less than desirable qualities. Everyone does.

He continues, "Yeah, pretty much. It's just been me and him for a while now so we look out for one another." He shrugs as if it's the most normal thing in the world and goes back to picking up some of the flowers.

"That's really cool that you have each other." I pause, thinking about how nice it must be to have a close-knit family . . . to know there is always someone there to look out for you.

"What about you? Are you close with your folks?" He gets up to dump two handfuls of flowers in the trash and reaches out for the ones I'm holding. I think back to when I was younger and how my dad would never let me ride my bike without a helmet, even though all the "cool" kids didn't have to. He would tell me it was because he wanted to protect me and didn't want anything to ever hurt me. I trusted him, so I wore it, even though I got made fun of. I silently scoff to myself. *Yeah, but you didn't exactly protect me from your own lies, did you?*

I shake my head. "Um no, well, yeah. I mean I was. Sort of. My parents died in a car accident about five years ago so now it's just me."

I try to avoid talking about this. Not only do I not like to think about it, but I hate to make other people feel uncomfortable. An awkward silence usually follows with mumblings of how sorry they are. I know it always comes from a good place, but I don't like when people feel they have to say something cliche. I also know it's best to leave out all of the other details of what happened, because that's just a whole other shade of complicated.

Without missing a beat, though, Lucas responds with "That must suck. It's gotta be hard not to have them around." He continues to deposit the broken flowers into the trash and then moves to mop up water with some more towels I have stashed under the sink.

I'm stunned by his realness and how he doesn't get all weird on me. So stunned, in fact, that I actually allow myself to admit out loud, "Yup. It really sucks. Part of me still hopes they can somehow see all I've done and where I live." I glance around the messy kitchen. "Well, maybe not in the state it's currently in, but you know what I mean."

He pauses and looks directly at me for a moment before asking, "Do you really believe that they can? Still see you, I mean." I stare right back at him, our eyes locked.

I'm startled by the sudden intense shift this conversation has taken. "I dunno. I guess I never really thought about it seriously." I search his face to try and gauge what he's getting at. "Why, what do you think?"

He gets that intense look again. "I don't know." Then, with a blink, Lucas breaks the moment and goes back to mopping up the remaining water. Not liking the heavy feeling in the air, I, too, return my focus to picking up more flowers.

After what feels like a profound moment of silence, he clears his throat and thankfully changes the subject. "So, do you always take off your clothes before you meet a guy, or am I just special?"

Jeez, this guy sure knows how to go from zero to flirty in a matter of seconds.

He grins at me from across the room and I blush at the memory of our very intimate introduction. Technically I guess it's not the first time I saw him, but I'm not about to admit that and sound like a total creep, mooning over some guy before I even spoke to him.

I prefer to keep the mood light now, too. I'm not sure what came over me before. Talking about my parents is not something I do—not even with Kelley, let alone someone I just met. But I've decided I already really like playful Lucas, so it can't hurt to indulge in a little harmless flirting.

"You're special alright." I chuckle and shake my head. "I'd hate to bruise your ego, but maybe I like to take my clothes off just for the fun of it. You happened to get a free show out of the deal, but in all fairness, I didn't even know you were coming."

He chuckles. "You're killing me, Kins," he whispers as he shakes his head. Then he looks up and says in the most sinful voice, "How about this—next time I promise to let you know before I come." It's more a promise than a question and I lose all feeling in my tongue. I really hope I don't drool right in front of him. Thankfully, I'm a master at hiding my true emotions.

"Deal." I unashamedly stare right back at him and give him my best flirty grin. This guy is good, and I'll be damned if I don't keep up and serve it right back to him. I'm definitely attracted to him and, from his confidence, I get the sense he's the kind of person who could be up for a good time. No strings attached, of course, which is fine by me.

He crosses the room to pile up the dirty towels when he suddenly stops to look at a few paintings I have leaning against the wall.

He picks one up and examines it closely before asking in a quiet, curious voice, "Where did you get these?"

I shrug. "I found them in the crawlspace when I was cleaning up the other day. A previous tenant must have left them here, but I thought they were so beautiful I couldn't bear to get rid of them. I thought I'd hang them up, I just need to get the right hardware to do it."

The three paintings are all landscapes filled with colorful fields of flowers, which of course I found extremely fitting to display in my place. You can tell the artist was taking great care in painting each stroke to really show the details. They aren't completely finished, and the corners are tattered and dirty, but something about their imperfection makes them even more beautiful to me.

Lucas gently puts the canvas he has in his hands back on the floor and takes a step back. For a second he looks startled, as if he's just seen a ghost or something. But he quickly recovers and goes back to focusing on cleaning up.

After a minute he casually adds, "I could help you hang them up."

That's kind of . . . random. I mean what guy willingly does manual labor for a girl he barely knows?

Maybe he just feels obligated as my stand-in landlord, but I certainly don't want any pity-help.

"It's nice of you to offer but I've already taken up enough of your time. I can handle it, but thanks anyway."

There, I've given him an easy out so he doesn't have to be held accountable for me.

He shrugs. "I have some picture hooks at home so I'll come by tomorrow."

Apparently it's not up for discussion.

I'm still down on the floor picking up the last of the flowers when he extends his hand toward me. Still holding onto a single flower, I reach up and place my hand in his as he helps me up to stand in front of him.

"I think that about does it. Place looks good as new, except for all your ruined flowers. At least this little guy looks to have made it out ok." He gently caresses the petals on the stem in my hand and I find myself becoming jealous of a damn flower.

"Yeah, it's a resilient little ranunculus," I mutter, still staring at his hand.

"A what?"

I snap my eyes back up to his. "A ranunculus. That's what kind of flower this is."

"Ranunculus?" He says it more as a question, as if maybe he heard me wrong. I nod. "Wow, that's . . . ridiculous." He laughs and drops his hand. *Damn.*

"Hey, I didn't come up with it. It may be a ridiculous name

but it's actually my favorite type of flower. The whorls of petals are so delicate and intricate, it's like a complicated maze of layers that you could get lost in. Yet when you step back and look at it as a whole it makes something completely amazing and beautiful." OK, so I totally just geeked out on a flower, but I can't help it—I find them to be so beautiful and interesting.

I remember being about four years old picking flowers in my yard. We lived next to a meadow and all of these different wildflowers would grow. I would sit there for hours, picking one of each kind and pulling apart the stems and petals trying to figure out how something so beautiful magically appeared out of the ground.

I can feel my cheeks start to turn pink when Lucas looks at me with genuine understanding and says, "When you put it like that I think it just might be my favorite now, too."

I extend the white blossom to him. "Then here. Why don't you take this one?"

He hesitates for a beat before reaching out and gently taking the stem from me. "I think this is the first time a girl has ever given me a flower."

"There's a first time for everything, mister. Now don't say I never gave you anything."

"Damn, first I get to see you half naked and now you're giving me presents. Kinsley, you might just be my new best friend."

I keep my eyes trained on Lucas as he grabs his leather jacket. He flashes one last smoldering smile, accompanied by a suggestive wink, before heading for the front door. I trail behind him and watch from the entryway as he walks to his car. He gives a small wave as he ducks into the driver's seat, and as I'm standing here smiling—and feeling pretty damn smug and proud of myself—I'm hit with a sudden realization.

Wait, did I just get friend-zoned?

CHAPTER

seven

Kinsley

"A LITTLE TO THE LEFT. Now back to the right a smidge. Almost there . . . maybe a tad higher?"

"Jesus, woman. You're kind of a perfectionist, aren't you?"

I cross my arms. "Hey, you volunteered to help, remember?"

I was actually surprised when Lucas showed up this morning, toting two coffees and a box of donuts. Part of me thought I completely misread everything that happened yesterday. I thought it may have been just me that felt some sort of physical attraction, but he seems to be just as flirtatious this morning. He likes to tease me—a lot—but he has been very patient with my demands for the pictures to be perfect.

He stretches to keep his balance as he adjusts the largest of the paintings. "Well I didn't realize it would be such an ordeal. You owe me big time, babe."

Feeling bold, I answer, "I'm sure I can think of a few ways to repay you."

For a split second he looks shocked that I said that, but smirks as he takes a step back so we're standing side by side, both examining how all three canvases look together. I decided to put them right in the front room so they are one of the first things you see as you walk in.

Without taking his eyes off the paintings, Lucas says, "Can I ask you something?"

"Sure."

"Why do you care so much about these? I mean, they aren't even finished."

I shrug, arms still crossed. "I don't know. I guess I like feeling some sort of connection to this place's past. Whoever painted these had some sort of story to tell and I hate to think they didn't get to finish it, that these were just forgotten in some dirty crawl-space. Maybe by my hanging them up it doesn't seem so sad." I laugh nervously when I realize I just admitted all that out loud. Thankfully, I stop myself before admitting my biggest fear is that I'll open my heart up only to end up alone and forgotten, with nobody to care about how my story ends. No, better to keep my emotional distance, no matter how easy it is to share things with Luc. Instead I try to lighten the mood by asking, "Does that sound completely crazy?" I drop my arms and turn to look at his face, which suddenly seems very serious. It makes my insides turn to goo.

He turns to look back at me. "Maybe a little. But I like that."

Our bodies seem to naturally shift a little closer together— so close I wonder if he can hear my heart beat faster in my chest. There's something about this man that gets me worked up. I try to attribute it to my intense physical attraction to him. But there is a small voice inside my head that keeps whispering *It's different . . . you like him.*

Shut up. No I don't.

OK, maybe a little . . .

I find myself wanting to know more about him—where he works, what he likes to do for fun, where he comes from . . . but I have to stop myself from asking too many questions. I've already opened up more about myself than usual in the two short times we've interacted. Something about him is just so comfortable I can't help it. But I need to keep myself in check. *Getting to know each other isn't important. Just hook up and get it over with so you can get him out of your head.*

Just as I think he's about to kiss me, we are both startled by the door.

It's a client of mine here to discuss flowers for her wedding. She's always about a half hour early, and while normally it doesn't bother me in the least, today of all days I wish she could have just been on time.

Or even better, extremely late . . .

I lead her back into the sitting area where Lucas is gathering up his jacket and keys. Lucas and I both stand quietly, neither of us making a move to say goodbye. Finally I hear Brittany clear her throat and I realize how awkward this must seem. "Oh, uh, Brittany, this is Lucas." I almost add '*my friend*,' but decide against it. "Lucas, this is Brittany."

"Nice to meet you." Lucas smiles his usual charming, sexy smile at her, which makes her blush and giggle. I have to fight the urge to remind her she's engaged, which is an odd, territorial reaction for me. But then Lucas looks back to me and says, "Well I guess I should get going."

"Yeah, I guess so." Except I really just want to beg him to stay, which freaks me out even more.

"See you later, Kinsley." And with that he saunters calmly out of the cottage.

Thankfully Brittany launches right into her most recent pile of photos and magazine clippings, stealing my attention away from what might have almost happened with Lucas.

CHAPTER

eight

Lucas

IT'S BEEN THREE DAYS SINCE I last saw Kinsley and I think I am losing my fucking mind. I can't even count the number of times I've picked up my phone to call her, but then stopped myself when I realized I would probably end up sounding like a toolbag. I don't want to come off as over-eager, so part of me hopes she will call me with another problem at the cottage just so I have an excuse to see her. And then I feel bad for wishing her to have problems. What a messed up sick and twisted roller-coaster of emotions.

The thing is, I just can't get her out of my head. And it's more than just being turned on by her, although that definitely plays a part. It's like the moment I noticed her at the wedding something in me *clicked* on. I just can't quite put my finger on what. And then when I had to come to her rescue with the sink incident?

Who am I kidding?

She sure as shit doesn't need anyone to rescue her. All on her own, she's fun, confident, sexy . . . and the way she flirts with me? Damn it if she doesn't make me want to break my no sex streak.

But there's more to my attraction than just the physical. There's something deep and mysterious about her, yet at the same time I recognize a familiar guardedness. I can tell there's more going on under the surface, and I want to know more about the girl inside. Nothing serious or anything, but I could see myself getting to know her in all sorts of ways . . .

"Earth to Lucas! Come on dude, where's your head at?" Ryan punches me in the arm. We're playing a two-on-two pickup basketball game in the park with our friends, Tristan and Logan, who also happen to be twin brothers.

"Sorry, man. Just thinking about some shit." I try to focus as Tristan checks the ball to me and I send it back.

"What's the matter? So much pussy that you can't think straight?" Tristan teases.

No, there's only one pussy in particular that has me confused . . .

"Yeah, we haven't seen or heard much from you in a couple of days, so we assumed you were otherwise occupied," Logan interjects with a wink. Much like Ryan, Tristan and Logan love to bust my balls. They are both big players—even by our group's standards—often using the twin thing to their advantage. They don't understand how I could willingly take a hiatus from the sex game, so they prefer to pretend I haven't.

T passes the ball to Logan who then heads toward the basket where Ryan is waiting to block him. I stay back and hold my arm out to cover Tristan.

"Just busy at work. If you actually showed up half the time, you would know that, wouldn't you?" I throw back at Logan, perhaps a little too much on the defensive.

Logan and I are also business partners for our company, GS Ventures, and we both live by the 'work hard, play hard' philosophy. We do our own thing so it's not uncommon for us to be traveling or working from home. We each also do our fair share of taking time off, but the work always gets done. It's really not fair for me to jab him like this, but hell, like I said I'm losing my mind.

"I bet this might have something to do with a certain new tenant of your father's," Ryan cocks his head to the side as Logan passes the ball to Tristan and he goes in for a layup. *Swish.* Another win for Team Trogan.

I bend at my waist with my hands on my knees, suddenly winded even though I didn't exert myself much. Just thinking about Kinsley makes me feel short of breath. After a beat, I join the guys at the picnic table adjoining the basketball court and take a swig from my water bottle.

Ryan chimes in. "Come on, Luc. Last time we talked you mentioned helping out your dad's new tenant, and then I didn't hear from you for three days. I met Kinsley at the lease signing, and I have to say, she seemed intriguing. And your dad seems to have taken a liking to her, too, so spill." Sometimes I swear Ryan talks to my dad more than me.

"What's there to tell? Yeah, I went over to help her because she was having some trouble with the sink. She wasn't wearing any pants, we joked, and I helped her clean up." I try to act nonchalant, as if this sort of thing happens to me everyday. *Jackass.*

"Wait, what? Back that train up, man. Let's start with her not wearing any pants." Tristan leans forward and rubs his hands together as if he can't wait to hear this story. In fact, they all lean in. I sigh. Here we go.

"She called in a panic because the sink was leaking so I went over to help. She was soaking wet and had taken off her pants to get changed, not knowing I was coming over. I happened to walk in on her, but she was cool as fuck about it and we even exchanged some jokes about the whole thing. I helped her clean up the mess and hang some paintings and we got to talking."

I try to explain it in a way that doesn't make me sound like A. A jerk, or B. A sissy. "I don't know, she's fun and down to earth and it was nice to have an actual conversation with a girl. She makes me laugh. She's also got her shit together and seems really independent. We became fast friends, that's all."

I look up from the water bottle I was subconsciously focusing on as I recounted the basic points of my time with Kinsley. Three sets of eyes stare back at me, and then Tristan bursts into a deep chuckle.

"Shit, Luc. You've got it bad for this chick, huh? Sounds like she's got you pussy whipped already," Tristan says through his amused laughs.

"Whatever, man. I just think she's cool and fun to hang out with." I lean back, avoiding eye contact.

Tristan rolls his eyes and mumbles "Yeah, OK."

I can tell he's not buying it, so I follow up with, "Well it doesn't hurt she's hot, either."

OK, I know that makes me sound like an asshole, but I don't feel like catching shit for this right now. I love these guys like brothers, but they aren't exactly experts when it comes to relationships that require more than pure physical attraction. Now is not the time to bring up the fact that she gave me a flower, which was the sweetest fucking thing I've ever been given.

Man, now I really do sound like a pussy.

Tristan continues to joke, which makes his brother laugh. Thankfully Ry has my back. "Maybe it's about time we all try to find a woman that's worth getting a bit more serious about.

We can't just fuck around forever, right?" He leans back as if he's being chill about the whole thing, but I know him enough to understand he's really saying that he approves of Kinsley and thinks I should go for it. We rarely have to spell out our feelings to each other. Bro code and all that. We have a subtle, mutual understanding. I nod back in response.

"Dude, you sound like the fucking Yoda of relationships or something." Tristan, not persuaded, punches Ryan in the arm. "We know you of all people won't get serious, so that's a load of crap."

Ryan shrugs, as if he was purposely making fun of the situation. "Yeah, but it sounded like some deep shit, right?" He reaches into his duffle bag before tossing something my way. "But still, better safe than sorry."

I catch the small square of foil and snicker as I realize it's a condom. Apparently Ryan really does think I should give things with Kinsley a shot. He winks before getting up to sling his duffle over his shoulder.

"As much as I'm enjoying our little hen party, I've gotta get going. I'll see you ladies at the shindig tonight."

We each mutter our own comebacks while fist bumping and single-arm hugging our goodbyes.

I DON'T FEEL LIKE GOING to this party, but considering our firm just forked over two million dollars for DSGN, our latest client, to launch their new mobile marketplace, I sort of have to make an appearance.

While I may not be feeling it tonight, I'm excited to see this company take off. When I first met the company's founder, Erik Evans, a year ago, he impressed me with his idea to create a modern, curated, online marketplace for designers to share their work and potential clients to browse for designers that might best meet their needs. It's a brilliantly crafted site that has advanced sorting features and a clean layout, with a high standard of what gets showcased to ensure only quality work gets posted. It promises to aid both the designer and the client looking for solid work, and I think both advertisers and investors alike are going to eat it up.

Evans has worked hard on everything from his business plan to his team, so I know I can trust him to follow through. He's willing to put in the effort to see DSGN become successful, which is a top quality I always look for in a CEO—dedication.

I pull up outside the tall building right in the middle of the downtown area and toss my keys to the valet. I hit the button for floor twenty-six in the elevator. We expect DSGN to expand quickly, so we decided it was best to get them a big enough office to grow into. I step into the lobby and notice quite a few people are already here. The party is spread out amongst the various offices and conference rooms. I make my way across the floor to find the bar. After the week I've had, I could seriously use a beer to take the edge off. Since it's still technically a work function, I won't get crazy, but one or two drinks can't hurt.

I find the bartender in the largest conference room to my left and order a bottle of Yuengling. Just as I'm about to take my first swig I feel a delicate hand grab my bicep.

"Hey, Lucas. I was hoping you'd be here tonight."

I look down at the expectant brown eyes staring at me from behind long, fake lashes. "Hey Chels. How's it going? Erik treating you well, I hope."

Chelsea (yes, my ex) is Erik's assistant, which means I've been seeing her more often lately. When I first met Erik he was looking to hire someone, and at the time Chelsea needed a job so I recommended her. I think part of me still subconsciously feels guilty for how things ended and this was somehow a small way for me to make it up to her. Despite our past, she's smart and qualified, and fits in great with the DSGN team.

"We were certainly busy getting ready for tonight, and I think he's nervous about how it will go, but he's still a great boss to work for." She looks out at the gathering crowd, then back at me before adding, "Now that this party is actually happening, though, I could sure use a break tonight to have some fun." I think I see her subtly rake her eyes down to my crotch, but when I blink she's just smiling up at me sweetly. She knows we're just friends so I must be imagining things. I really am off my game lately, and it's messing with my head. I don't know what else to do but smile awkwardly back.

Thank fuck Ryan and Logan choose this exact moment to come over and say hi. I give them each a nod and slide myself away from Chelsea. She just as casually moves close to my side again, seemingly using the other people hovering and waiting to get drinks as an excuse to be so close. Is this always how it is with us? Why all of a sudden do I find it to be so damn uncomfortable?

Logan gestures around the room. "This place looks great. I'd say this company has a real shot at being one of our best investments to date. Erik was just showing me the newest beta version of the site and it gets better every time I see it. I know I fought you on this at first, but maybe you've still got it, Graham." He takes a swig of his beer and shoots me a taunting grin.

"Gee thanks, Sharp. I try and earn my keep around here." I, too, take a drink of my own beer and look around. The place is pretty packed, a good sign that word is getting out. Chelsea grabs my arm as someone behind her pushes in to order a drink. I try to keep the conversation going with the guys so I don't have to focus on her. "So where's T? Think he got lost on his way over?"

"Oh, he's here. Free food and booze and a chance to meet

women? Like he'd pass that up!" Logan scans the room for his brother and points over to the side. "He already met some chick he's hot for and looks like he's trying to make his move."

I look over to where Logan is pointing and see Tristan cornering some woman against the wall. He's got his classic "player face" on—the one where he tries to act all charming and sweet while really just trying to get into a woman's pants. I shift slightly to see who his poor victim is and suddenly I can't breathe. *Kinsley.*

Dressed in a simple black dress with her long brown hair falling casually around her shoulders, she instantly has my full attention.

"Fuck," I mutter under my breath. Ryan must hear me and realize who I see because I hear him utter a barely audible *Shit* as well. Suddenly my legs have a mind of their own, and the next thing I know I abandon my beer at the bar and am heading straight through the sea of people scattered about the room until I stop right next to Tristan and Kinsley. I go for a playful slap to Tristan's back, although it comes off harder than it should. "Come on Sharp, stop harassing my friend here."

There I go using that "friend" word again. Why does is suddenly sound so lame?

What I really want to say is *"Get the fuck away from my girl,"* but, A. She is not my girl and B. I'm trying really hard not to scare her off.

"Friend?" Tristan looks utterly confused as he glances between me and Kinsley.

"Yeah, this is Kinsley. She's renting my dad's cottage. He entrusted me to look out for her while he's gone, so that certainly means keeping her away from the likes of you." I smile at Kinsley to let her know I'm joking (except I'm not). Tristan looks between us once more, then gets a big shit-eating grin on his face as he realizes who she is. Our conversation from earlier today rings in my ears and I narrow my eyes at him as if to say *Yeah, that Kinsley. So keep your mouth shut and walk away before I have to kick your ass.*

He must take the hint, because he says "I see then. Well, Kinsley . . ." He says her name real slow and deliberate, simultaneously shooting me a subtle, teasing glance. " . . . if you've got this guy in your corner you're in good hands. Luc here is nothing if not true to his word. If he told Papa Graham he'll look out for you, you're as good as taken care of." And with that he leans back, literally backing off.

I could fucking kiss Tristan right now.

He winks at Kinsley—*OK maybe I should punch him again instead*—and then smirks at me before turning to leave. I slide a little closer to Kinsley and lean down to say, "Sorry about him. He's mostly harmless, but he can be a bit of an ass. Hope he didn't give you a hard time."

"Nah. I could've handled him. But thanks for looking out for me, *friend*." The way she says "friend" like that makes me want to kick my own ass for being the one to say it in the first place. Before I can even begin to apologize, she follows up with, "So, tell me. In addition to being my own personal handyman *and* bodyguard, what other benefits does being your friend come with?" She raises a questioning eyebrow and the most devilish grin plays across her lips. This girl is good. She always manages to surprise me and I frigging love it.

Two can play at this game, though.

I reach out and brush a strand of hair off her face before leaning in close, putting my mouth dangerously close to her ear as if I'm about to reveal the dirtiest little secret. She lets out a small gasp and I hear her hold her breath as her pulse quickens. "I also happen to make a really mean grilled cheese." She continues to hold her breath for a second, then lets it all out in a burst of full on laughter that makes her eyes light up.

Well, isn't that just the best fucking sound ever?

I join in with my own chuckle as I realize the ridiculousness of my statement, but the plan was to throw her off. By the way she can barely breathe from laughing so hard, I'd say mission accomplished.

She finally starts to compose herself. "You're crazy," she says playfully.

"And you're beautiful."

OK, that was probably a little out of line for me to just blurt out, but I can't help it. It's true.

A smile breaks out across her flushed face, but then she looks down as if embarrassed by the compliment.

I move to stand right next to her and lean my back against the wall, stuffing my hands into my pockets. I'm afraid if I keep them out any longer I'll be too tempted to touch her hair again.

Why did it have to be so fucking soft?

Changing the subject, she asks, "What are you even doing here?" She turns to look at me sideways, resting her head against the same wall I'm leaning on.

I grab my chest and feign an offended expression. "Wow. That hurts. Am I not cool enough to be at this kind of party?"

Just when I think she's going to reply with some snappy comeback, she simply shrugs. "I'm just surprised to see you is all . . . in a good way."

I can't resist the way she blushes.

"My company invested some money into DSGN to help get it up and running."

"Your company?" she asks, confused yet intrigued.

"Yeah—GS Ventures. My buddy Logan and I started up a capital investment firm a few years back. We like to help new companies get off the ground."

"Really? I had no idea. That sounds like an amazing job."

"It can be. It's a lot of risk, but I love to see things grow from nothing into something." Kinsley mulls that over, and while she looks like she has about a million questions she wants to ask me, she just nods. "So what brings you here, then?" I ask.

"My friend Kelley works for Burton Realty and I guess they helped you guys find this office. She invited me to come, although she seems to have disappeared." She glances around the room trying to locate her friend. "Oh there she is, talking to Ryan by the bar." She smiles to herself, as if she knows something I don't.

"Oh right, you met Ryan when you signed your lease."

"Yeah. Wait . . . you know him, too?" Before I can even get a word out she puts some of the pieces together. "I guess since he's your dad's lawyer you would know him, huh?"

"That, and he's my best friend. That's actually *why* he's my dad's lawyer. We grew up together so he's like a second son. There is nobody my old man would trust more than Ry with his affairs."

We fall into a comfortable silence as we both look out around the crowded room. After a minute or two Kinsley turns to me. "Wanna play a game?"

I look at her intrigued. "What kind of game?"

"Hmm . . . how about twenty questions?"

I'll bite. This could get interesting. And friends should get to know each other better, right? "Only if we both get to do the asking."

"Fair enough. I'll go first. How old are you?"

"Twenty-eight. How old are you?"

"Twenty-five." She stands up a little taller, as if used to defending her young age.

"Really, you're only twenty-five? You really seem to have

your shit together for being so young."

"I could say the same thing about you, Mr. Graham. Favorite color?"

"Blue." I don't mention the fact that I specifically mean the exact shade of her eyes. "You're going easy on me, I see."

She looks at me, tilts her head up, and crosses her arms, challenging me. "Fine, I take that one back. What are your three biggest turn ons?"

Now we're getting somewhere. I turn to fully face her and run my hand through my hair before answering. "Well, one is the way you just asked me that. Two would be seeing a woman in nothing but a sexy pair of underwear and a wet shirt, completely unaware of how gorgeous she is, and three would be meeting someone who is extremely smart and surprising and can make me laugh. You?" She just stares at me, processing what I just admitted. *It wasn't too obvious all three things were about her, right?*

She mulls that over for a second before she starts ticking off her list, using her fingers to indicate each trait. "The first is confidence. Second is having my neck kissed, and third, I can't resist a guy in a suit."

I look down at my own black pants, white button up shirt, and black jacket, then meet Kinsley's gaze. Before I have a chance to fully process what she said, she shoots right back with "Have you ever been in love?"

Damn, so much for the easy questions.

I stare at her for another long second before dropping my head and shaking it slowly. "Nah. Maybe I thought I was at some point, but I don't think it was ever for real."

Now it's my turn to play dirty. "When's the last time you had sex?"

She looks up as if thinking about it before standing up straight. "I guess it's been a while." She then looks me square in the eye before asking what turns out to be the game-ending question: "Want to help fix that for me, *friend?*"

And to think I didn't want to come tonight.

CHAPTER

nine

Kinsley

LUCAS RAISES HIS EYEBROWS IN a mixture of amusement and excitement before grabbing my hand to pull me through the packed room.

I'll take that as a yes?

I wasn't lying when I said I was surprised to see him here tonight. It's been a few days since he helped me with the paintings, and since I hadn't heard from him I figured I really was misreading his intentions. But then he practically forced his friend away from me tonight and picked up right where we left off.

He has such a way of making me feel out of control, I figure the best way to counter that is to gain the upper hand. Ever since we met I felt some sort of connection, and, as crazy as it sounds, I already feel so comfortable around him. Like I can be myself. We can go from serious to joking to flirting in a matter of seconds and he doesn't seem to judge me. He just rolls with it, which is refreshing and fun. There is clearly some sort of undeniable chemistry between us, and I figure if we just get this physical attraction thing out of the way I can go back to my normal life where every thought isn't consumed by him. I bet we could be friends—friends with benefits, even—and not let it get weird. He doesn't seem like he's in any rush for a commitment either.

He maneuvers us through the crowd and turns right into the hall outside the conference room. The party is spread out amongst the various offices, and it seems as if all of the rooms are filled with people drinking and talking. We keep moving further down until Lucas takes a sharp left down a quieter corridor. Finally we reach the last office on the left and he pokes his head in to make sure it's empty. He pulls me inside and closes the door behind us. I hear the click of the lock before I turn around to face him. The light from the hallway is diffused through the frosted glass windows of the office, casting a dim, seductive glow throughout the room. Lucas takes a hesitant step closer to me before stopping again. He intently studies my face, as if trying to read my thoughts. To let him know it's OK, I move toward him. I reach my arms up to his chest as he moves his own hands to my shoulders. Our faces are so close I can feel his warm breath on my skin.

"Are we really going to do this?" he asks in a husky voice.

There is something about the ambiguity of the way he says *this* that makes me wonder if we're on the same page, so I decide to clarify. "It's just sex, Lucas. As friends. No strings. I'm not looking for a relationship, so as long as you're not, either, we're good."

He moves his face toward mine as confirmation, his hands sliding to cradle my neck as our lips connect. I'm surprised and overwhelmed by how *right* his mouth feels on mine that I'm pretty sure I let out a moan. My eyes roll to the back of my head. He runs his hands through my hair and gently pulls me closer.

I grab at his dress shirt and try to pull him even closer to me. Our mouths move quickly, hungry and desperate. Next thing I know he is walking me backwards until my thighs hit against the desk. As I perch my ass on the edge, using it for support, Lucas moves his hands to clear a path for me to scoot back. I hear papers and pens clattering as they get pushed aside before he removes his suit jacket and tosses it to the floor, his lips never leaving mine.

I feel a strong, warm hand caress my left leg from my knee up to my thigh, then it moves under my dress, grabbing my hip. He uses his left hand to grab my right knee and gently forces it aside so he can stand between my legs. Still gripping my hip, he pulls me toward him in a possessive move. I can feel how hard he is against me. His . . . *package* . . . is practically bursting through his pants. I decide now would be a good time to help him with that. *And maybe help myself.*

Like an overeager child unwrapping a present on Christmas morning, I reach down to grab his belt and quickly move the strap through the metal buckle, pulling back to release it. Our mouths still connected, I yank it all the way off with one hand as I reach up with my other to grab his shoulder. *Sweet Jesus, his biceps are perfectly sculpted and solid.* I get the top button of his pants undone and slide down the zipper when he grabs the sides of my face with both hands and leans his forehead against mine, breaking our heavy make-out session.

I analyze his face to make sure everything is all right. His eyes are still closed and he is caressing my cheeks with the pads of his thumbs. He takes a deep breath before looking up and locking his gaze directly on to mine. "You're killing me, Kins." I open my mouth to ask what I did, but he silences me with another heart-stopping kiss. I take that to mean everything is still good, so I press my lips back to his just as hard.

I move my hands to undo each of his shirt buttons. Once I'm done with the last one I take the opportunity to admire his six (*more like eight!*) pack abs with my fingertips. I catch a glimpse of a tattoo on his right side, stretching across his ribcage, but further inspection will have to wait until another time. He slips his hands back under my dress and grabs both sides of my lace panties. He takes a small step back and glides them down my legs in one swift motion before dropping them to the floor. He places one hand behind my head and the other grips my waist as he gently lays me back on the desk. He trails soft kisses down my neck, no doubt recalling my little admission from earlier. *The man is good.* As if I couldn't get any wetter . . .

He must know this, because I barely have time to process the whole neck kissing thing before I feel one of his strong fingers push inside me.

I let out a small gasp as he works his finger in and out, then stretches me a bit further with another. Still moving his hand rhythmically, his mouth makes its way back up to mine. He kisses me deeply before whispering, "You're so perfect and wet for me" against my lips. He then leans back to stand up and slowly—oh so *sloowwwly*—slides his fingers out from me. I perch myself up on my elbows and watch as he stares at me. I scoot myself up to reach for his pants again, which are totally in the way right now. Lucas quickly reaches into his pocket for his wallet and pulls out a foil packet. I slide his pants down his strong legs and I'm pretty sure I involuntarily lick my lips at the sight of him.

OK, maybe it's voluntary.

He grabs himself and strokes up and down a couple of times before tearing open the condom and sliding it on. It must be obvious I'm gawking at him because he lets out a small chuckle, puts his hand behind my neck and says "Lay back, babe" as he maneuvers me back down on the desk.

Mmm . . . bossy Lucas . . .

I do as he says, and once he seems satisfied that I'm comfortable, he positions himself between my legs and pulls me to the edge of the desk by the backs of my knees. He moves his right hand back up to grip my hip, and uses his left to guide himself inside me. He goes slowly at first, until I adjust to his size, then starts quickening his pace. Now both of his hands grab my hips and I reach out to grip his forearms, silently praying this will never end. Sex is usually a way for me to escape, and most of the time I'm left feeling more empty than satisfied.

But this, right now, with Lucas?

It's hard to describe, but it's as if he's holding me so close that all of my broken pieces are fitting perfectly back together. I throw my head back and squeeze my eyes shut, afraid to open them in case it all turns out to be a dream.

How much time passes? I'm not quite sure. Seconds? Minutes? Hours? I am in such a state of ecstasy that I lose all concept of time and space. I finally brave opening my eyes to look up at Luc and find him staring right at me—right *in* me—and it's in that moment that I lose every ounce of control as a wave of complete and utter satisfaction rolls through me. I let out a moan and relax back against the hard wood of the desk. I don't let go of Lucas' arms, but my grip loosens. When I'm done riding out the intensity of this feeling, I feel Lucas shift closer so his mouth is at my ear. "I'm gonna come, babe . . ." he whispers—clearly remembering his promise when we first met—before falling apart a second later. He drops his head to my chest as he stills inside me, and we lay there, each trying to catch our breath. I think I feel his lips on my skin before he pulls back and picks up a box of tissues that previously had been knocked to the floor. If I didn't know better, I'd say it was a gentle kiss, but he's up and cleaning himself off so fast I'm sure I must have imagined it.

I sit up, holding onto the edge of the desk to ground myself. My legs dangle off the side and I watch as Lucas pulls his pants back up. He looks over at me as he stuffs his hands in his pockets. *God he looks hot standing there with an unbuttoned white shirt.*

I also think he looks nervous, but then he quickly lightens the mood by saying "So . . . was it good for you?" with an adorable tilt of his head and a small shrug.

I'm not sure how to read him now, so I decide to play it safe and shoot back with my own playful shrug. "It was OK. Very *friendly* and all." I smile so he knows I'm teasing.

He chuckles and drops his head. One hand moves to rub the back of his neck. "Well, glad I could be of service."

He gets that nervous sort of uncomfortable look again, and then starts to button up his shirt as if to keep himself busy.

Hell if I make this awkward. I mean I was the one who basically just asked him to screw me out of the blue, so I want to reiterate that I don't expect anything more.

I *can't* expect anything more.

I jump down from the desk, smooth out my dress, and reach down to pick up his jacket. I hold it out and he takes it from my outstretched hand. "I guess we better straighten up." I look at the assorted office supplies scattered on the ground. I lift up a name plaque from the floor and glance at the name. "I'm sure Mr. Evans wouldn't be too thrilled that we just got it on in his office." I begin straightening the items that were pushed aside.

Through a lopsided grin he theorizes, "If anything, I'm sure he'd just be jealous."

I throw what I hope is a flirty smile over my shoulder. "It can be our little secret, then." I throw in an exaggerated eyebrow wiggle for good measure. Lucas starts to laugh, so I know my plan to amuse him worked. "Come on, let's go grab a drink. I'm parched." I reach for the door and gesture with a nod for Lucas to follow me.

"Aren't you forgetting something?" Lucas looks down at the floor where a black scrap of lace is still laying.

I shrug my shoulders. "Nah. They're all wet. I hate wearing wet underwear. Let's just say it can be a little consolation prize for Mr. Evans. Secret be damned." I wink as he bends down to pick up the panties, holding them out on one finger.

"You're crazy, Kins." He shakes his head, but I can tell he's entertained.

I slide the fabric out of his hand and smile sweetly. "And you love it, Luc."

WE MAKE OUR WAY BACK out to the party when Kelley suddenly runs up. "There you are! I thought I'd lost you."

"Sorry, Kell. This is Lucas, Eli's son. Lucas, this is my friend Kelley." I motion toward the elevators. "Luc and I just went outside to get some fresh air." I glance at Luc, who nods at the introduction looking cool as a cucumber. Maybe he does actually want to keep this a secret.

"I'll let you two catch up. I'll grab us some drinks." Luc smiles at us both before heading off to the bar.

Kelley watches him walk away and I fight the urge to poke her eyes out. Thankfully she turns back to me a second later.

"Wow, Kins. That's Eli's son? No wonder you're always breaking shit at the house." She nudges me and I can't help but laugh. On our way over tonight I mentioned in passing how Eli's son helped me with a few things, but I didn't offer up too many details.

"I do not break shit there . . . not on purpose anyway. And Luc and I are just friends. He's being really nice helping me out while his dad is gone."

"Yeah, *Riiight.*" I don't even have to look at her—I can sense the eye-roll in the tone of her voice. Whatever.

I attempt to change the subject. "You're one to talk. I saw you with Ryan earlier."

"Yeah. It was just business. Trust me, I don't see that going anywhere else, which is a shame because he still smells goddamn delicious." She shakes her head, disappointed. "It seems we have a few new clients in common though, so I'm sure I'll be seeing more of him."

Kelley then starts to talk about a few deals they are both working on, but I can't hear her. My mind is suddenly focused across the room where I see some leggy blonde with fake lashes grabbing Lucas' arm and whispering something in his ear. I'm too far away to make out anything that they say, but from the way he smiles and lets her lead him out of the room, I think I get the gist.

Ever since my parents died, I hardly ever have the urge to cry. It's like I'm broken and can't feel things right anymore. But right now I can certainly feel the tears prick the back of my eyes, which is making me all sorts of confused. I know I was the one who proclaimed our hookup to be no big deal, but from the way my chest aches and my stomach turns, maybe I don't know what the heck I want. Clearly he didn't take what just happened to mean anything more than what I said it was—a fun time with no strings attached—and why should he?

And just like that I am reminded that relationships are not my thing and I shouldn't pretend sex with Lucas was anything more than just that. I haven't up to this point, so what in the hell made me suddenly get so emotional? The tears that were starting to well up immediately subside.

It was just a quick hookup, albeit a really mind-blowing one, but a casual hookup none the less. Sure I like the guy—in a strict-ly have fun with a friend kind of way—but that's it. I stand up a little straighter and purposely look away from the direction Lucas and the blonde went. The only way to handle this is to maintain control.

If I decide to leave feelings out of this, I can't get hurt.

CHAPTER

ten

Lucas

SO.

Fucking.

Intense.

That's all I can say about sex with Kinsley. I'm no stranger to being with a woman—many women in fact—but it has never been even close to this. The way our bodies seemed to fit together so perfectly, the way her skin felt on mine, the way her lips tasted . . .

Damn, I need to pull it together.

I was just trying to get a rise out of her when I asked about the last time she had sex. I mean, she started the damn game. But when she propositioned me, I couldn't help myself. To hell with celibacy. She made it clear she's not looking for a commitment, so if we can have a mutually *friendly* relationship, then why the hell not? Thank God I saved that fucking condom Ryan threw at me.

I replay the moments over and over again in my head as I walk over to the bar. Part of me thought she was all talk, and when we were alone she would just laugh and say "Gotcha," but from the moment our lips connected, I was a goner. She's definitely a woman who knows what she wants and isn't afraid to get it. I was so stunned by what happened—and how she didn't try to make some big deal about it—that I could barely say anything to her afterward. Good thing Kelley came up to us, because I was about five seconds away from dragging Kins back to the office for a repeat performance.

Or to just hold her close, because I think I would be OK with that, too.

Oh for the love of fuck . . .

I could use a minute alone to process.

But no sooner than I go to order a drink, I feel a hand on my arm. *Chelsea.* Just perfect.

"Hey stranger. I was wondering where you wandered off to."

"Hey. Yeah turns out my . . . uh, friend . . . showed up so I went to say hi." I try to avoid making eye contact. I don't want to deal with this right now.

"Your friend? By the way you couldn't keep your eyes off that girl, I'd say she's more than just a friend. And even if she isn't yet, my bet is she will be soon." Chelsea gently pats my arm and gives me what looks like a genuine smile. Discomfort and confusion must show on my face, because she starts to laugh and leans in so only I can hear. "Oh, come on, Luc! You don't think I believe you're a hermit now, do you? I get that you need to get out there and play the field, so to speak. You can tell me about the women in your life. We're friends, right? " She looks at me sweetly and I can't help but smile back. Maybe Ryan has misjudged her feelings.

"Now come on, Erik has some people he wants to introduce you to." She steps back and grabs my arm to pull me into the next room.

AFTER WHAT SEEMED LIKE THREE hours of schmoozing and shaking hands last night, I was finally able to break away from Erik to go look for Kinsley. But unfortunately Ryan told me she had already left. It was late so I didn't want to call her, deciding instead to see if she would be around this morning.

I pull up to the cottage and see a black Honda parked in the drive. I walk up to the porch and knock on the door. After a minute, a surprised looking Kinsley appears. She offers up a smile, but something about it feels forced.

"Hey. I was hoping you'd be here. Sorry I got pulled away last night."

"Oh, no worries. I saw you were . . . occupied." She makes no move to open the door.

"Yeah, Erik wanted to introduce me to some people so I had to do the whole work thing. I still owe you a drink, though."

"Don't even worry about it." She just stands there shifting her eyes as if she's a bit uncomfortable. The way she doesn't ask me to come in makes me feel completely shut out . . . literally and figuratively.

"Can I come in?"

"Sure." Kinsley opens the door and steps aside before turning down the hall. "I'm just working on a few things in the back."

I follow her to the back room where she begins to busy herself with an arrangement of flowers on the big worktable, her back to me. A slightly awkward silence ensues as I try to figure her out. Is she mad? Full of regret? She seems more indifferent than anything else, and I'm not sure what to say. I keep thinking back to how she didn't want last night to be a big deal, so maybe she thinks I'm the one who's going to be weird about it.

"Listen, Kins . . . I'm not really sure how to do this whole friends thing, but I like spending time with you. You make me laugh and you keep me on my toes, yet you're also really easy to talk to. And what happened last night . . . it was pretty great." I try to keep my voice steady and cool so as not to give away the fact that I actually think what happened last night was fucking amazing. "I was thinking maybe we could see where this goes?"

Kinsley drops her head before turning around to face me. "I like spending time with you, too, Luc. I like that it's easy. My life is crazy enough right now and I don't need any drama or complications. I told you I'm not interested in a relationship, but I just want to make sure we're on the same page. If we are to continue anything here, it would be strictly a friends with benefits type situation. Nothing serious."

I take a step closer so I'm leaning next to her at the table. Despite the fact that I have an undeniable attraction to Kinsley—a physical one as well as some type of emotional one—I also know that I am crap when it comes to real relationships. I don't want to hurt her, so the fact that she is the one shutting me out of the emotional side is almost too good to be true.

"Not only are we on the same page, I think we both wrote the same damn book." I chuckle as a more genuine smirk breaks across her face. "Let's just say I'm not exactly looking for anything serious, either."

We both stay quiet for a second. If she hadn't just told me herself this was going to be casual, I would swear she looks sad. But then she smiles and says, "Good," so I'm wondering if it's only me that feels strange about it. I was just offered the perfect situation, so I shake off any feelings of . . . what is that?

Disappointment? Nah. I think I'm just in shock. I basically get to have my cake and eat it too, if you catch my drift.

I relax my shoulders. "So, now that we've established we're pretty great together, does this mean we can continue to explore our *friendship* further? You said yourself you like easy, and babe," I drop my voice low and seductive, "I'm *always* easy."

She laughs before nudging me in the shoulder. "Oh yeah? Well you might not want to go spreading that little fact around there, pal. People will talk."

God, her smile is gorgeous . . . Wait, friends can still think that kind of shit, right?

I turn and move to stand in front of her, resting my hands on either side of the table behind. I put my lips impossibly close to her ear. "It can be another one of our secrets then." I look into her eyes to make sure she really wants to see where this goes as much as I do, and next thing I know she's grabbing onto my shirt and her perfect mouth is on mine.

I catch both sides of her face and kiss her deep. I'd be lying if I said I wasn't feeling all sorts of pent up and ready to throw her down and take her right on the table. But I see her flowers perfectly arranged in their vases, so I opt to grab her ass, spin her around, and walk her backward. I feel like a fucking animal, but that's what this woman does to me.

With her back pushed against the wall, I reach for her shirt and pull it up over her head. She's wearing the sexiest black bra that makes her boobs look fucking edible. I can't help but go in for a handful of each, kissing across her chest. She reaches for my shirt and I help her pull it over my head. I feel proud of the way she looks at me with pure lust in her eyes.

I go for the button on her jeans just as she reaches for mine and we both scramble as if it's a race to see who can get the other's clothes off faster. Kinsley moves her hands up around my neck and her hips start grinding against mine. She's in only her black bra and matching boy short panties and it's taking every ounce of my self-control not to come before I even get inside her.

And then reality hits me like a punch to the throat.

"Fuck," I groan, kissing Kinsley one last time before pulling back. She lets out a cute, pouty breath. "I really hate to have to say this, but I don't have a condom on me. I used the only one in my wallet last night and I didn't exactly plan for this to happen when I decided to stop by. Are you on the pill?"

She continues to hold onto me, looking unsure. She gently pushes me back before saying, "Yes. But I think I have some condoms in the bathroom."

She returns a minute later. I can't help but kiss her again, this time taking my time to really taste her. Everything seems to slow down, and our previously frantic need for each other now seems less hurried, but just as desperate.

I slide her panties down her smooth legs and run my hands back up the sides of her calves and her thighs. I roll the condom on before lifting her up so she can wrap those gorgeous limbs around me, arching her back into the wall for support. I cup her ass, holding her up, and gently push inside her. The second I feel her warmth suck me in, I swear I see stars burst behind my eyes. How it is possible to feel so fucking good, I will never know. It's like her body was made for mine.

I hold her tighter as I increase our rhythm, and her soft, breathy moans against my ear are shooting straight to my dick. Afraid I won't be able to hold out much longer, I begin kissing Kinsley's neck and whisper, "Let go for me, Kins," to which she responds by holding on a little tighter as she explodes in my arms. I follow right after, my face buried in her neck, trying to breathe all of her in.

I stand there panting, still holding her up. She takes a long, deep breath before going still. "Hey now, don't fall asleep on me. You'll wound my ego if it wasn't exciting enough for you." I chuckle into her hair.

"Maybe you'll just have to try harder next time." I can feel her smile into my neck.

"At least you admit there will be a next time."

"If you're lucky, maybe." She gently pushes herself away. "But for now I really should get back to work."

"Seriously? No cuddling, or anything? You really are the perfect girl." I joke as she starts to gather her clothes.

I meant it to be funny, but the way she rushes to put her jeans and sweater on without some snappy comeback makes me feel like an ass. The sad truth is I would cuddle the hell out of her if she wanted me to.

After getting dressed, Kinsley busies herself with a couple of arrangements, and watching her work is pretty damn captivating. She gets this serious look on her face and unwittingly bites her bottom lip as she looks out at the flowers laid before her. It's the same look she had when I first saw her, and it's even more enthralling up close. She very thoughtfully grabs a stem and adds it to the vase, then adds another and another until this amazing display appears before her. I don't know the first thing about flower arranging, but she makes that shit look good.

Not wanting to disturb her concentration, I leave her to it and spend the afternoon puttering around, helping to fix up a couple things around the cottage that I noticed need work. I probably should leave to get some of my own work done, but I want to spend some time with Kinsley. I don't know what we're doing, but I sure as shit want to stick around to find out.

The next thing I know the sun is starting to set so it must be after seven. I gather up my tools from tightening some loose boards on the porch and make my way to the office.

Kinsley is on her laptop, engrossed in whatever email she's working on.

"Ready to call it quits for the day? I'm starved and could go for some food. Or maybe have you again."

I lean against the doorframe with a seductive look in my eyes, but she barely acknowledges that I'm standing here. For a minute I wonder if she even heard me.

I take a step closer and lean down to stick my head above the laptop screen opposite her.

"Hello? Earth to Kinsley." I go for playful, waving my hand to get her attention.

She finally glances up with a half-hearted smile, then goes right back to typing away. "Sorry, just finishing up some stuff. Did you need something?"

"Just you, naked and willing." She looks stressed, so I figure a little flirting will ease the tension.

But again, she barely nods her head, still too focused on the computer screen to respond. Jesus, this woman knows how to put up walls. It's as if she just shuts the world out and stays locked in her own head. It's admirable that she is such a hard worker, but frustrating she won't take two seconds to acknowledge what's right in front of her. I've seen her serious and thoughtful as well as playful and feisty, but this is just sad. I get she might feel over-whelmed by running a business and being on her own, but she deserves to let someone else in once in a while. I feel like I catch these amazing glimpses of her letting loose, but then she goes right back to closing up.

Looking for a reaction, I slide my hand over the laptop to close it.

She looks shocked before sharply asking, "What are you doing?"

"I'm helping you out of your own head. From the looks of

it, things are pretty intense in there. I think you could use a distraction. Maybe grab a bite?"

I assume the way she crosses her arms and looks all indignant is supposed to intimidate me, but really I just find it cute as hell.

"Come on, Luc. You've done enough. You don't have to stick around or anything. I'll be fine. I'm good on my own, I promise. You don't owe me anything. I can get my own dinner."

Forget the wall—this girl has built up a goddamn fortress—moat, dragon, and all. Looks like it's time to come blasting through with a fucking cannon.

"Damn it, Kins—loosen up, will ya? I'm not asking you to fucking marry me or anything, I'm just trying to feed you."

She looks embarrassed by my lack of subtlety. It's then I get an idea, so I quickly follow up with, "Look, do you trust me?"

Her eyes narrow and she skeptically studies my face. I think I see her head make the slightest nod, which is good enough for now. I extend my hand, and while she hesitates for a second, she finally places her own in mine so I can pull her toward the door.

"What are we doing?" She sounds nervous, but continues to let me lead her through the front door to the driveway.

"Something crazy. You'll love it." I wink just as I open the passenger door on my Gran Coupe and motion for her to get in.

CHAPTER

eleven

Kinsley

AS WE PULL INTO THE lot of the country club, I wonder what in the hell we're doing here. Maybe Lucas is a member and he's just taking me for dinner like he talked about. Now that I know he's well off with his impressive venture capital firm, it would make perfect sense. I've been here a couple of times to set up flower arrangements for fancy weddings, but I've only ever used the small service entrance in the back. I know the place is majorly swanky and I suddenly feel very underdressed in my jeans and light grey sweater.

As Lucas gets out of the car and opens my door for me, I try my best to play it cool.

"So, are we here for dinner?"

He smiles before squeezing my hand and leading me toward the entrance. "Something like that."

"I don't think they'll let me in dressed like this." I motion to my rather casual attire. He, himself, is only wearing jeans and a white t-shirt.

"You look perfect. Just go with it."

Just as I'm about to protest again, we waltz up to the hostess stand in the lobby. Lucas flashes his gorgeous smile at the man standing guard by the double doors. By the way the guy eyes Lucas from head to toe and smiles back just as big . . . well let's just say *I'm* not exactly his type.

"Hey Derek, " Lucas says, clearly ogling Derek's little gold name tag. "My friend and I are here for the Thompson engagement party." He nods toward a big, white, framed sign that notes in large, flowy script:

Thompson & Carroll Engagement Party,
Right Wing Terrace

Derek gives us both a once over, clearly appalled by our current clothing situation. I give Lucas the evil eye as if to say *"See, told you so."*

Lucas, as smooth and calm as can be, adds "I went to college with good ol' Thompson. This guy's seen me passed out naked in the middle of our dorm hall, so trust me, he'll consider me overdressed for the occasion."

Another charming smile from Lucas, and Derek looks like the visual alone is enough to satisfy him. I can practically see him snapping a mental picture. I actually think I see Lucas blush under Derek's stare, but before I have a chance to point that out, Derek is motioning toward the door saying "Right through here, then take a right down the hall."

Lucas thanks him and guides me in the indicated direction.

As we walk down the hall my mind is going about a million miles a minute. "Wait, you're taking me to your friend's engagement party?"

"Nope."

We make it out to the terrace where about two hundred people dressed in fancy suits and dresses are milling about, sipping glasses of champagne and accepting the tiniest hors d'oeuvres from silver platters being carried around by about a dozen waiters.

I glance around the party, trying to understand the connection. Lucas looks like he's about to burst as he holds back a smile.

"Oh my God. You don't know Thompson at all, do you?" The mildly horrified—but also impressed—look must show on my face, because Lucas no longer even tries to hide his amusement as he shrugs. "We're seriously crashing this party?!" I try to keep my voice low and my excitement contained, which only makes Lucas smile brighter.

"Hey, what better way to blow off some steam than a place where nobody knows us and we can pretend to be anyone we'd like? Plus there's free food and booze. How can you say no to that?" He nods toward the bar, which sits next to a large buffet. "And if you really want, I'll even let you leave your underwear somewhere inside."

I lightly shove his arm. "You really are crazy, you know that?" I can't help but smile.

"Takes crazy to know crazy."

Lucas looks at me with pure excitement in his eyes, which is rather contagious. The thought of being here when we shouldn't is exhilarating. He seems to get that I sometimes need to let go and live in the present moment. It makes me wonder if he's just doing it to one-up my sex-on-the-desk proposition, or if he has his own past that needs escaping, too.

After being with Lucas so intimately for a second time, I'm still not sure how to feel or what to think. I continually let my guard down around him, knowing it's only going to end badly in the end. I want to keep up this cool, casual vibe, but I can't seem to squash these stupid *feelings* from forming so I instinctively push him away and shut down emotionally.

He practically jumped at my offer for no strings sex, so why he stuck around today is really sort of baffling me. And the fact he actually took the time and effort to care what I'm thinking . . . to actually get frustrated enough to force me to talk to him? What's up with that? We established we're simply friends with benefits, but he seems to be just as enthusiastic about the friends part as the benefits part.

It's only a matter of time before he gets bored and moves on to the next girl (something he had no problem with the night of the party), so for now I'm just trying to enjoy this—whatever it is—while it lasts. No matter how much I know it will never go anywhere, I can't help but like how Lucas makes me feel when we're together. Sometimes it is nice to let go, even if it's only on a physical level.

If nothing else, Lucas can provide me with a temporary escape from the loneliness I've been feeling lately. I know it will be short-lived, and then it's right back to being in-control Kinsley.

But for tonight it *would* be nice to feel like I don't have to be myself for a change.

AFTER AN HOUR OF STUFFING our faces and trying to remain inconspicuous, Lucas and I finally make our way back to his car. We made sure to keep our distance from the soon-to-be bride and groom, and, despite a few disapproving looks, thankfully the rest of the guests were too refined to bother ratting us out.

The grin on my face must be about a mile wide, and when I see the way Lucas looks at me, I suddenly wonder if I have something in my teeth.

"What? Did I act like a total idiot and give us away in there?" I bite my bottom lip as I lean against the car door.

"Nah, I'm sure most of them don't even know their own names by now, let alone know who we are . . . or aren't. Besides, I left a very generous monetary gift, so if I had to guess we'll even be seeing an invitation to the wedding real soon." Lucas stands in front of me, sporting his own pleased look. "Did you have fun tonight?"

"As much as it shames me to admit it, yeah, I really did." I pretend to bow my head sheepishly, but still can't keep from smiling. "I'm sorry I was caught up in my work earlier and forced you to take such drastic measures, though."

"Hey, if you can count on one thing, it's that I will always be there to call you on your shit. That's what friends are for, right?"

"Thanks, Luc. I mean it. I'm used to being by myself, but it was nice to get out and forget for a bit."

"Forget?" His brow furrows with concern.

What I want to say is that for the first time in a long time, despite being in a strange place full of strangers, being with him made me forget the constant loneliness I usually feel.

But thankfully I realize how incredibly stupid that would be, so I opt for a normal response. "Just . . . everything. Work, bills, you know . . . the usual for everyone."

He nods his head as if he understands, despite looking like he wants to push further. But rather than throw it back at me, he follows up with, "Yeah, life can get pretty heavy sometimes. It's a real bitch. But the way I see it, we should just have fun while we can and figure the rest out as we go along." He simply shrugs.

I find the way Luc sees the world strangely comforting. He calls it like it is and I can't help but wonder if he's so cool and collected because it's just his attitude, or if something from his past caused him to be so mellow. Maybe a little of both? I can see how his carefree attitude and sometimes crude humor can come off as immature, but I sense it's just a front. It's like I can see something much deeper going on when he gets that intense stare of his, but he's very good at keeping it bottled up. He's able to brush everything off and be spontaneous. I admire that, as it's something I myself also desperately try to do.

I almost give in to asking him about it all when, after a silent pause, he adds, "I guess I should get you back home. As much as I've taken great pleasure aiding in your corruption, I know how much your work means to you. Just promise me you'll remember to let loose sometimes."

I shake my head, silently scolding myself for almost losing it. We both move to get in the car and I go for being playful—being safe—instead. "You mean like propositioning men to have sex at office parties and crash fancy parties at the country club?" I raise an eyebrow to him as I buckle my seatbelt.

He puts the car in gear before looking over to meet my eyes with a lustful spark. "That's my girl."

CHAPTER

twelve

Lucas

"Why didn't you write me? Why? It wasn't over for me. I waited for you for seven years, and now it's too late."

"I wrote you 365 letters. I wrote you every day for a year."

"You wrote me?"

"Yes. It wasn't over. It still isn't over."

"ARE YOU FUCKING KIDDING ME?" I'm sitting next to Kinsley on the couch, watching Ryan Gosling and Rachel McAdams suck face in a rainstorm on the TV.

Kelley, who is sitting on the other side of Kinsley, tosses a pillow my way. "Shut up, you're ruining the best part."

I roll my eyes. "I'm just saying . . . these movies set up an unrealistic expectation. I mean this dude built her a fucking house *after* he knew she was engaged to someone else. How can any guy compete with that?"

Kinsley giggles from her seat between us. It's been a week since we crashed the engagement party and we've settled into a comfortable type of companionship as we both keep things easy and detached. There has been a silent understanding that we each have our reasons for doing so, but the more time I spend with her I can't help but want to know more.

We've either seen each other or talked almost every day this week, so I stopped by tonight thinking we would hang out. But she forgot she already had plans for a movie night with Kelley. I was going to leave them to it, but Kelley invited me to stay. I'm not sure how much Kinsley has told her about us, so I've been on my best behavior.

Kelley pokes Kinsley. "Come on Kins, back me up. It's romantic. A grand gesture and all that."

"Sorry, Kells, I'm with Luc on this one. It is a bit dramatic."

Kelley pinches Kinsley's leg. "You're a bad judge. Just because you don't believe in love, doesn't mean you have to ruin it for the rest of us."

This makes me sit up straighter to look at Kinsley. "Really?"

She shrugs and looks back to the movie.

Kelley chuckles from the other side of the couch. I continue staring at Kinsley but she refuses to make eye contact. Kelley must pick up on the vibe shift because she looks toward Kins, then toward me, and smiles to herself before sitting up to put on her shoes.

"I should get going. I've got an early day tomorrow, so no time to sit here and argue about this with you two cynics." She gives Kinsley a quick hug and makes for the door. Before she leaves she looks over her shoulder and says, "I can see why you two might get along." And with that she closes the door behind her, leaving Kinsley and I alone.

Kinsley grabs the remote and clicks off the TV. "At least now we don't have to finish this."

I know she's talking about the movie but I pretend she means our discussion. "Nice try. You're not getting off the hook that easily."

At this point I'm amused. Our situation doesn't exactly lend itself to deep talks about true love and all that, so seeing her squirm is entertaining. I know I'm playing with fire, but I want to know everything going on inside her head.

She sighs. "What? Come on, I would think you of all people would understand me. You said yourself this movie is a load of crap."

I can tell there is a story here and I'd be lying if I said I wasn't curious as hell to find out what makes this girl tick. "True, but I never said I don't believe in love. The way it is portrayed in this movie, yes. But in general? I think it exists."

She looks confused, like I just shattered everything she thought she knew about me. Before she gets the wrong idea, I clarify. "Don't get me wrong, it's not for me." She visibly relaxes. "But I've witnessed it. My old man loved my mom more than anything, so I know that shit is real."

"Then why isn't it for you?" She asks slowly, as if struggling with whether or not she wants to know.

I take a deep breath. I'm not sure at what point we're crossing a line of appropriate conversation, but for the first time I feel like I can trust a girl enough to understand. She clearly has her own issues when it comes to relationships, so maybe, just maybe, she might relate to mine.

"My mom died when I was thirteen. Cancer. She got really sick and I watched the hell both she and my dad went through. My dad is strong, though. He got through it and still manages to stay optimistic about life but I know it tore him up. One of the last things my mom said to me was that she hoped I would someday find someone to love as much as she loves me and my dad. But when she died I told myself I never wanted to have to go through that pain. It must have stuck."

Kinsley turns to sit cross-legged on the couch next to me. She pulls a pillow into her lap like a shield and hugs it gently. "At the party you said you thought you were in love once."

It's more an acknowledgement than a question, but I'll take the bait.

"A few years back I dated this girl for a while. Chelsea. Things got pretty serious but I just wasn't ready for a commitment. I realized if I could be with someone for five years and still have no desire to be with her forever, my love gene must be fucked. That's why I really hope my mom can't see me now. If she can, she must be pretty pissed I'm incapable of doing the one thing she hoped for."

I shrug coolly, trying not to show that I feel ashamed. Ashamed that I couldn't give Chelsea—or my mom—what she wanted, and ashamed that I often act like an asshole to hide it. Truth is I *want* to love someone and have them love me back. I want what my parents had, but I know it will only bring pain and heartache so I pretend I don't care. It's easier that way.

"Chelsea and I are still friends, but I feel bad I wasn't able to give her more. Maybe someday things will be different, but for now this is who I am."

I decide not to add that I already feel closer to Kinsley than I ever did with Chelsea. *I* don't even understand that one, so I'm sure as hell not going to confuse her with it. We agreed this is strictly a friends with benefits arrangement, which is best for everyone involved.

But, benefits aside, I genuinely like having Kinsley as a friend.

She looks lost in her own thoughts. Just when I think she's going to open up about her own past, she tosses her pillow at me. "Look on the bright side—at least you don't have to worry about any of that with us, right?"

She stands up, heading toward the kitchen. Apparently sharing time is over. "Yeah," I call after her, gripping the pillow. "Good thing."

All of a sudden I'm overcome with a sense of empathy for Chelsea. I suddenly know how she must feel to have me keep her close, yet shut her out.

Yes, it's a good thing I don't have to worry about Kinsley and I being the same.

Good fucking thing . . .

CHAPTER

thirteen

Kinsley

THE NEXT COUPLE OF WEEKS fly by as I keep busy with lots of orders. I've been saying yes to just about anything that comes my way. Anniversary bouquets? Of course. Corporate parties? Sure! Funeral arrangements? Yeah . . . I do that now, too.

I keep telling myself it's only for the money—and the love of it—and it has nothing to do with trying to avoid thinking even more about a certain someone than I already do.

Ever since our movie night, Lucas and I have avoided serious conversation topics, which is for the best. When he opened up and told me about his mom and his past, I could have sat there all night and listened to him share every last detail of how he got to be the man he is now. I could tell he doesn't let many people in on the more intimate aspects of his life, and I feel really special he trusted me. I came close to spilling my own story, but after I heard him talk about Chelsea, something in me shut down again.

For some unexplainable reason, I hate that he thinks he's broken. Even if I don't believe in love, I can tell he still does. The fact he believes in it but thinks he's incapable of having it makes me feel very sad for him. It also kills me that he feels like he's disappointing his mom. I can tell by the way he talks about his parents that they had something very special, and even if it's in sharp contrast to my own screwed up familial experience, I can't stand the thought of him somehow ending up like me. I can't let him self-destruct by pushing people away. I've already lost everyone so it's too late for me, but he hasn't. He still has a father who would do anything for him and a woman who's loyal.

Speaking of, I'm sure if there is any *friend* who could help fix him it would be Chelsea, a girl who apparently still stands by him even after he ended their relationship. I'm just a fun stop along Lucas' track to finding love . . . a convenient, peripheral distraction to help pass the time.

If I was smart I would end things now so he could get out there and find something real, but the selfish part of me isn't ready to let him go. I've convinced myself that maybe I'm helping him forget his past just as much as he's tried to help me forget mine. After he left that night, I decided if there is one thing I can do for Lucas, if I care about him at all *as a friend,* it's to help him realize he's doesn't have to be defined by his past. He can change, if he wants to. He doesn't have to be like me, so closed off from love. I know my life isn't meant to be shared with someone else, but he showed me that he still has hope, which I admire. And I'll be damned if I let him lose that.

Lucas has also been busy at work these past two weeks, but we've been texting during the day and hanging out most nights when he stops by the cottage. Snippets from our text conversations look a little something like this:

LUCAS: *What are you wearing?*

ME: *Nothing at all. I just hang around my place naked all day. Perks of being my own boss and all.*

LUCAS: *Seriously? That's just not fair . . . I don't think Logan would like it if I started showing up to work buck ass naked. Pics, please?*

ME: *Nice try. You want it, you gotta come get it. ;)*

LUCAS: *Be there in ten.*

LUCAS: *Make it five.*

ME: *The window is stuck again. Do you have the number of the guy your dad had fix it?*

LUCAS: *No, but I can find out. Or you can just try to find a video on YouTube to fix it yourself. ;)*

ME: *You think you're clever?*

LUCAS: *Hell yeah—I'm fucking funny!*

ME: *Well maybe I can find some other handsome man that will come to my rescue while you're busy laughing.*

LUCAS: *Like hell you will. I'll grab some pizza and be there around 8. I'll fix the window. Don't even think about calling anyone else. Promise?*

ME: *OK fine, I promise.*

LUCAS: Good morning

ME: Morning :)

LUCAS: What are you up to today?

ME: Working, as usual. I have a lunch meeting with a potential new client and then I'm delivering some flowers to the Windsor Hotel around 3.

ME: And you, Mr. Big Important Investor Man?

LUCAS: I've got back to back meetings until 6, so I won't have my phone on me.

ME: OK. I'll be sure not to bother you then.

LUCAS: You never bother me, babe. I want to see you though. Can I take you to dinner tonight?

ME: Sure—it's a date.

LUCAS: I was hoping it would be ;) I'll pick you up at 7.

Wait . . . what does he mean by that last part? He's hoping it will be a date—like a *date* date? Did I even mean it to be that kind of date?

Or maybe he's just glad to have his friend agree to a casual dinner after a long day.

Ugh. Maybe this whole friend-helping-a-friend thing will be harder than I thought . . .

I GET BACK FROM DROPPING off the flowers at the hotel a little after four, and since it is right near Kelley's office I decide to stop in and say hi. I haven't really seen or talked to her since the infamous movie night—I've just been so busy with work and Lucas.

I enter the Burton Realty office and nod to Gemma, the eager, young receptionist. "Hey Kinsley! How've you been? Congrats again on your new place. I saw the pictures and it looks gorgeous!"

"Thanks, Gemma. I'm pretty excited about it. Is Kelley here?"

"Yup, she should be in her office. Feel free to head on back."

I thank her before heading back to the third office on the right.

"Knock, knock . . ."

"That can't be my best friend, could it? I've just about forgotten what she looks like." Kelley tries to hold back a grin, so I know she's not *too* mad at me.

"Yeah, I deserve that." I plop down into the chair in front of her desk. "It's been a crazy couple of weeks."

"I know, I'm just messing with you. It's hard being such an in-demand lady boss. I feel lucky you've taken the time to come visit."

"Oh please, you know I love you. I just finished dropping off an order and now I have some time to kill. What better way to spend this lovely Friday afternoon than to distract you from work."

I try to act casual, but Kelley immediately picks up on my implied admission. "Time to kill? Is something going on tonight?"

Time to come clean, I guess. I feel bad I haven't told Kelley about me and Lucas, but I think part of me is scared of how she'll react. I know her view on love and relationships, so I don't want to disappoint her. I could really use her perspective on this whole situation now, though, because I'm not sure what's happening.

"Um, Lucas is taking me out to dinner." As soon as I say Lucas' name I see Kelley's grin widen and she gets that *Told you so* look on her face. "Just as friends . . ." I quickly follow up with. "I think . . ."

"You two are still sticking with this whole friends story, huh?"

"Well, it is true. Mostly. We hang out and talk and watch movies and stuff. It's just . . . well . . ." I blush just thinking about screwing Lucas on some random person's desk. "Let's just say I do some things with Lucas that I never do with any of my other friends."

"I knew it. You guys totally had sex, didn't you?" Kelley leans forward and rests her chin in her hands, as if she can't wait to hear this.

I look up to the ceiling, avoiding eye contact, and blow out a deep breath. I finally muster up the courage to look at Kelley and shrug innocently. "Maybe?"

"Maybe my ass! I felt something weird going on the night we watched the movie, but as soon as I first saw you two together at that party I knew something was up. Wait! Is that when you did it?!" I feel myself blush again, which is all the confirmation Kelley needs. She picks up her phone and dials a few numbers. "Hey Gemma, hold my calls. I have an important meeting going on right now." She puts down the phone and points directly at me. "Spill."

I fill Kelley in on the past month, starting at the beginning when I first met Lucas at the cottage. I decide to leave out the part about noticing him at the wedding. I know that will just turn into some sort of musing on fate, which I don't hold much stock in.

Kelley sits quietly most of the time, nodding and smirking every once in a while. I finally get to the end, up until our plans for tonight.

"I don't know, Kells. The whole situation is confusing now. I like being around him, but just as friends. I thought I had things under control, which is why I didn't want to say anything, but now I'm not so sure."

Kelley relaxes back in her chair. "Honestly, babe, I think you need to just have a talk with him. Better get it all out on the table—or desk I should say." She winks, which makes me laugh.

"I thought we did talk. I made it very clear we are strictly non-serious friends with benefits. But sometimes I feel like that's not always the case."

"Seriously, Kins, it sounds like right now you have the best of two worlds. You have a hot guy to fool around with, as well as a friend to just hang out and eat pizza with. No complications, no attachments. And if that's what you're cool with, then far be it from me to tell you how to label it." I start to feel a bit more confident, as if maybe this little arrangement is fine as it is, but then Kelley leans forward again. "But can I ask you one thing?"

I should have known I wouldn't get away so easily. "Shoot."

"Are you guys still seeing other people?"

I chew my bottom lip for a second. I know I certainly haven't been. Not that any other guys are beating down my door, exactly, but to be honest, I really haven't even thought about wanting to see anyone else since meeting Lucas. I realize we never talked about being exclusive or anything, so who knows how many other "friends" he has? If the night of the party is any indication, he could very well have more.

The thought makes me feel instantly nauseous. "I know I'm

not . . ."

"I'd suggest you clarify that fact on his end, too. Because the answer might mean the difference between a casual, convenient hookup and something more." Her eyes soften as she reaches out to squeeze my hand. "For what it's worth, though, I think you deserve to have someone take care of you in your life. Someone you trust and someone you can count on. You know I'm always here for you without question, but someday you're going to have to let someone else into your heart, Kins. You haven't had the best luck with the men in your life, but I promise you not all guys are complete jerks. I know you don't think I'm the expert here, but you do deserve to be happy."

I squeeze her hand back, trying to keep myself composed. Kelley believes in holding out for Mr. Right, but up until now I never thought he existed. The part that scares me the most is that I can see Lucas being that person I finally let in, even a little bit. I can't expect to help him if I don't. How can he realize he deserves love if I won't trust him enough to open up? If that's the compromise I have to make to help him find happiness, then that's what I have to do.

I just wonder at what point we will be crossing a line we can't come back from.

Kelley gives my hand one last squeeze, pulling me out of my own deep thoughts. "Now, about this date . . . I say you better go get ready and put on something to make Lucas lose his mind. At the very least you know there's a good shot you'll get lucky tonight."

CHAPTER

fourteen

Lucas

I PICK KINSLEY UP AT seven and lead her to my car before driving us to *Pedro's*, my favorite local Mexican restaurant. It's not overly fancy, but the food is awesome and the vibe is casual. It's also a special place for me and a part of me wanted to take her here for that reason. When Kinsley opened her door and I saw how amazingly beautiful she looks tonight, I almost lost my shit. I had to keep my damn hands in my pockets to stop myself from reaching out and dragging her to her bedroom.

Her brown hair is pulled to the side in a loose braid, and she is wearing a pretty floral print dress, belted at her perfect waist, with an oversized cream sweater. She also has on these black stockings and when she got into the car I could have sworn I caught a glimpse of a garter holding them up.

She's so goddamned playful and cool that I feel like I must be insane (and a major lame-ass) for even hoping she meant calling our outing tonight a date in a more-than-just-friends kind of way. Ever since our more personal talk a couple of weeks ago, I think about her even more. If that's fucking possible. It felt . . . freeing, opening up to her, and I maybe want to see if there is anything beyond our casual friendship.

The drive to the restaurant is quiet. We're both lost in our own thoughts, but it's not an uncomfortable silence. I pull into the lot and we get out of the car to head for the door. "Hope you like Mexican."

Kinsley looks up at me and smiles. "It's my favorite." I hold the door open for her—yes, I am a gentleman—and we get a table for two.

I never really considered *Pedro's* to be romantic, but now, as I look at Kinsley sitting across from me, eagerly scanning the menu in this dimly lit place, her face illuminated by the single candle sitting on our table, I'm starting to wonder if this place really is perfect for a date. Hell, real date or not, I'm just glad to be here with her. For the past two weeks we've mostly been hanging out at the cottage when I get off from work, and while it's been fun, I feel like there is always some big giant fucking elephant in the room. It's been easy—almost too easy—and I've been waiting for shit to hit the fan. I'm not sure how Kinsley feels about us anymore, but all I know is she is the first thing on my mind each morning, and the last thing at night. We can flirt, joke, talk, fuck . . . all of which is great, by the way, but I don't know what she's really thinking. Hell, I barely know what I'm thinking, other than I can't *stop* thinking about the woman sitting in front of me.

You're in deep, dude.

Yeah, I know.

"So, what looks good?" Kinsley is still looking at the menu.

"You." I have to remember we're still keeping things casual, which means sticking to carefree flirting.

She looks up from her menu, eyes wide and wicked. "Too bad that's not on the menu." I start to argue that point before she leans in. "Maybe for dessert, though . . . if you're good that is" She winks and goes back to perusing the menu.

"Babe, you know I'm always good." I don't even try to hide the way I lick my lips and devour her from her eyes to her chest. Who am I kidding? I fucking AM ready.

Good thing the waiter chooses this moment to come take our orders, because all the images that just flashed in my head of what I could do to this girl on this table would probably rack up every single health code violation possible.

Kinsley orders the shrimp fajitas and I order the steak ones. The waiter nods at us before taking our menus and heading off to the back. We both sit in silence again.

"You know what I just realized?" Kinsley startles me with her question.

"What's that?" I take a swig of water.

She shifts to cross her legs and looks at me. "We never got to finish our game of twenty questions."

"Yeah, I guess we got . . . distracted." I smirk and raise my eyebrows. "Still have some burning questions for me, Ms. Moore?"

"Maybe a couple."

"For you, I'm an open book."

She pauses, collecting her thoughts. "Are you still sleeping with other women?"

We're not going to beat around the bush with bullshit, I see. Good.
"Since we . . . ? No."

I swear I see her visibly relax at my answer.

Suddenly I get very protective. "Why? Are you still seeing other guys?" The thought never occurred to me, but it instantly makes me want to punch someone in the throat.

She looks at me with sincere eyes. "No."

Thank fucking goodness.

It's my turn to relax back into the chair. I don't know what the rules should be, but I do know the thought of Kinsley with anybody else makes me fucking crazy.

The discomfort must show on my face, because Kinsley teases, "Why, you wouldn't be jealous, would you Mr. Graham?"

"Hell yeah, I would." I tease back to break some of the intensity of the thought of her with another guy. "Is that OK with you?"

Kinsley sits back and shrugs. The way she subtly furrows her brow in confusion has me quickly following up with "It's just a guy thing. We don't like to share." I smile, trying to keep things light.

But the really big shocker? I never get jealous. Ever. As I said, the girls I was with in the past were just warm bodies, only there for companionship, as harsh as that may sound. Even with Chelsea, I didn't obsess over what she did or her being with other guys. In the insanely short amount of time I've known Kinsley, though, I can't *not* think about her and what she's doing every single waking minute.

Our food gets delivered to the table, which is enough of a distraction to change the course of the current conversation. Two sizzling plates are put before us. Kinsley eyes hers with a look of pure anticipation that is cute as shit.

"This looks so good!" She practically moans.

"You won't be disappointed." I grab my knife and fork. "I love that the food here is so authentic, and you can count on it to always taste good. My parents and I used to come every Friday night. It's tradition."

Kinsley is busy piling shrimp and peppers and onions onto

her tortilla before she loads it with guacamole and sour cream. "Both your parents?"

"Yeah." I nod, taking a forkful of my own meal.

Kinsley glances up at me as if expecting more, so I chance continuing. "Before my mom got sick, it was our family night. It was always really important to her."

Other than having to explain that she died when I was young, I've never talked about my mom to any girl I've met, friend or otherwise. But something about Kinsley makes me want to tell her everything. It's not lost on me what a big fucking deal it is that I brought her here, to our family place, on a Friday night. My dad and I still come here together every week, and when he's away I come by myself.

Kinsley seems lost in thought. I wonder if that was too much to admit for our circumstances, but then she quietly says, "Sounds like she was very special."

"She was." I decide to go for broke. "As I said, I've never seen two people more in love than her and my dad. They drove each other crazy, but in the best way possible. She was always coming up with these ridiculous activities for them to do together, like tandem bicycle riding or cheese making or some shit. She said it kept things exciting." I smile at the memory of my dad on the back of a two-rider bike.

"Somehow I both can and can't picture your dad doing those things," she says with an amused giggle.

"Well he usually complained the whole way through, but he did them. If it made my mom happy, he would do just about anything. Although I suspect he secretly enjoyed it."

"What did she do for a living, your mom?"

"She was an artist . . . a painter. I used to hang with her out at the cottage while she worked, drawing in my own notebooks trying to copy whatever it was she was doing."

Kinsley stops eating and her eyes go big and wide. "The cottage was your mom's?" It comes out as a small whisper of a question. Then she realizes the real kicker. "And those are *her* paintings."

She states it as if there is no question, but I confirm anyway. "Yeah. She said she needed a separate space to be creative in and that it was the perfect place. Like something out of a fairy tale. After she died my dad and I decided to hold onto it, but kept it empty for years. Dad always got offers but was never interested in giving it up. That's why I was surprised he told me out of the blue he rented it to some smart, young business owner. He thinks you're really special, Kins, and I have to say, I'm glad it's you who's finally using that place again." From the way she looks genuinely touched I can tell it means a lot to her.

And the fact that she cares so much for a couple of unfinished paintings means a lot to me. More than she will ever know.

She shakes her head and busies herself with pushing food around on her plate. "No pressure or anything, right?" She looks up with a shy expression on her beautiful face.

I smile back. "No, none at all."

We both chuckle and since things seem to be going well, even though it's getting more personal, I decide to really press my luck.

I clear my throat. "So what about your parents? What did they do?" I ask offhandedly and continue to eat so my full attention isn't focused on her, thinking it might be easier for her to answer if she isn't completely put on the spot.

She stares at her fork. "My dad was a salesman. He travelled a lot. My mom did some odd jobs to keep busy, but never really had a career."

While not exactly giving me much to go on, I try to keep her talking. "Sales, huh? Is that where you got your business sense from?"

She looks sad, and I feel like I said something wrong.

"Um, maybe." She picks up a bite of food. "Hey, how did your meetings go today?" She shoves the fork in her mouth, and it's clear the topic of her family is no longer up for discussion.

I lean back, trying to assess what exactly made her shut down so quickly. But I also don't want to make her feel bad about it, so I tell her they went well and launch into a story about Logan trying to hit on the girl who delivered our food, which makes her laugh.

The rest of the conversation stays light, mostly small talk about things like if my dad is enjoying his trip and how business is going with *Petal*. Neither of us finish our food, and when the waiter comes to bring us the check I slip my credit card in with the receipt to pay. Kinsley tries to protest as she starts to take her wallet out of her purse, but I quickly shove the little black holder into the waiter's hands.

"I should at least pay half. Friends split bills, right?" Kinsley says with a questioning glance.

"Sorry, babe. When I ask you out, that means it's on me." Gentleman, remember?

The look on her face is a mixture of confusion and distraction before she mumbles a soft "Thank you." Despite not wanting to talk about her family, she seems different tonight. More vulnerable, a little less guarded or something. She's at least showing interest in getting to know more about me, which is some sort of progress. I like seeing another side of her. So far I've thoroughly enjoyed every single side of her that I've had the pleasure of exploring.

The waiter brings back my credit card and the receipt as Kinsley finishes off the last of her water. "So, what now?" she asks as I finish signing my name.

Good friggin' question.

I'm not sure what she means or what she wants, but I figure it's a good chance to go for it. I'm not ready to call it a night yet. "Do you want to come over to my place?" I ask, perhaps a little too hopefully.

Thankfully she returns a big smile. "I'd like that."

CHAPTER

fifteen

Kinsley

IF I THOUGHT I WAS nervous before dinner, then now I'm a complete wreck. I've never been to Lucas' apartment before, and after all the stuff I have to process after our dinner conversation, his car suddenly seems cramped. It's too small for both of us *and* all of my thoughts.

I'm glad I at least had the courage to ask him straight out about seeing other people. I'm not sure how I want to feel about his answer, but relief and skepticism are both definitely mixed in there. I convince myself it's because I don't have to worry about catching some weird STD or anything, although part of me doesn't even believe he's being completely honest. But, hey, at least I asked.

And even if I didn't fully broach the subject of my past, I let him talk about his. I'm taking some comfort he still seems to trust me. Plus, I genuinely enjoyed learning more about his family. Hearing that Lucas and Eli let me rent the cottage when it meant so much to Lucas' mom? Talk about feeling your heart skip a beat! And it's got to mean something that he shared his special family tradition with me, right? Maybe he's ready to let go of his past. Which, I remind myself, would mean our little arrangement will be over a lot sooner than I had originally anticipated.

I'm overcome by an overwhelming feeling of sadness at the thought, but I force myself to shake it off.

No, this is what is best for Lucas. And you.

By the time we pull into the garage of one of the more luxurious apartment complexes in town, I've regained some of my composure.

"Wow. I'm in the wrong business. This parking lot is nicer than most apartments I've lived in." I try to manage a light chuckle as I get out of the car, but I think it comes out as more of a rather unattractive snort.

Lucas comes around the side of the car and places his hand on the small of my back as he leads me through a set of doors to a large, fancy elevator. "I bought this apartment when we landed our first big client. I thought I was cool as shit. Turns out it's really just a complex full of people who are trying to overcompensate."

"Oh, yeah? And what are you overcompensating for?" I let my eyes roam down to his crotch, then look back up to him and raise a teasing eyebrow.

He looks at me with a smug, panty-dropping grin. "We both know it's definitely not that."

I want to make some sort of joke to wipe that look off his face, but damn it if he isn't right. I end up just shrugging my shoulders, avoiding his gaze as we ride the rest of the way up to the twelfth floor.

Lucas unlocks his door and motions for me to step inside.

To the right is a spacious kitchen that looks like it actually gets used. Fresh fruits and veggies sit in a big bowl in the center of a large island, and a glass-doored fridge showcases that it's stocked with more healthy looking food. Beyond the kitchen is a large living room with two leather couches and floor to ceiling windows on the far side. You can see the entire town lit up. There is a black dining table nestled to the left, and I can see two hallways leading off to both the left and the right.

I wonder which way Lucas' bedroom is . . .

"Can I get you anything to drink?" Lucas' voice snaps me from my lustful thoughts.

"I'm good, but thank you. I like your place," I say as I look around once again, this time trying to take in every detail.

For as big and modern as it is, the apartment still somehow feels very warm and comfortable, not cold or sterile. There are small touches that make it feel like a real home. In the living room there is a large gallery wall of family photos and paintings, each meticulously framed and hung. I recognize Eli and Ryan in a few of the photographs, and I see the same woman in many of the pictures. "Is this your mom?" I ask, leaning in to examine her features. Lucas has the same eyes.

"That's her." Lucas places his keys on the island in the center of the kitchen and grabs a bottle of water from the fridge. He leans back against the counter and takes a large sip before setting it down on the surface next to him.

He continues to watch me take it all in. I walk over and stand in front of him grabbing his water and taking my own long drink.

"I thought you said you were good?" He grins at me as he tilts his head to the side.

"I am." I place the water back down where it was. "So, Mr. Graham, now that you've got me here, what are you going to do with me?" I tease.

He chuckles and shakes his head while grabbing my hips to pull me closer. He takes a deep breath, leaning his forehead against mine. "What *are* we doing here, Kins?" He whispers in a more serious tone.

I gently press my hands to his chest, trying to push away but simultaneously needing to hold onto something. I hesitantly look up to his face, a little afraid of what I'll see. I want to help him, but I also don't want to lose him.

"We're being friends." I stare at him, hoping my face appears as calm and collected as I'm trying to keep it.

He looks straight back at me. "I'm trying real hard to just be your friend, Kinsley. Except I—"

Before he can get another word out, I press my lips hungrily to his. I don't know what he plans to say, but I know I'm not ready to hear it.

He kisses me back just as wild. I feel some sense of relief that we're still *us*.

Kissing Lucas never ceases to amaze me. It's as if he can always tell exactly what I need, when I need it. Until him, I never realized how much I appreciate feeling like I have someone to look after me, someone to be there. There is a part of me that wants so badly to just give in and open up every last part of myself to this beautiful man before me, but then there is the part of me that is programmed to put up walls. The part of me that knows nothing but pain and the part of me that fears I will eventually lose all of the people I try to love.

This is easier. This is what we're good at.

His hands tangle in my hair as he walks me back a few steps toward the dining room table. Thinking he's going to take me right here in the kitchen, I start to scoot back to rest on the edge of the table, but before I know it I'm being scooped up into

Lucas' strong arms and he's heading down the hall closest to us.

"Not tonight, babe. As much fun as I have with you on desks and against walls, I think it's about time we tried doing it in a bed for once."

I giggle. "If you insist."

His eyes get serious as he gently places me on a soft, king-sized bed. The lamps are off, but the city lights beyond the big window are enough to provide a romantic glow. "Yes, I do," he says in that sexy, seductive bedroom voice of his.

He leans down and kisses me, much softer and sweeter than before, but still just as passionate. His lips move slowly down my neck as he begins undressing me. He first pushes off my sweater, placing a soft kiss to each shoulder. He continues to rain kisses down my chest as he undoes my belt, then reaches to pull my dress over my head. Laying on his bed in my pink lace bra, matching underwear, black garter belt, and thigh high stockings, he pauses and stares at me. While he's seen me with far less clothes on, I've never felt so exposed. "God, you're fucking beautiful," he whispers as he reaches back down to run his hands up my sides. I crave how he looks like he can't get enough of me. I get off feeling like I can make him react that way.

I arch into his touch and pull him closer to me. Who am I kidding? *I'm* the one who can't get enough. He continues to kiss me all over as he works to unbutton his shirt and push off the rest of his clothes. Now naked, I can see exactly just how turned on he is. He takes his time unclipping my stockings and sliding my panties down my legs, then off comes the garter. He moves his fingers behind my back to unclasp my bra and soon I am completely bare before him as he stares at me hungrily.

I'm ready to beg him to jump on top of me when he kneels down and grabs my hips to pull my ass to the edge of the bed. He keeps one hand at my side, gently caressing from my hip to my ribcage, while the other makes its way between my legs. He slowly traces every bit of my skin to the point of madness before I feel his soft, warm, wet lips on me. His tongue expertly glides over my clit, while his fingers tease just below. Right before I feel like I could combust from desire, he plunges two fingers deep inside me and works them in a gratifying tempo, all while using that amazing mouth to bring me over the edge. I'm pretty sure I cry out—*loudly*—in pleasure, and I'm pretty sure I don't care. I've never been able to let go so completely before, and something tells me it has more to do with the man between my legs than holding back of my own volition. Lucas has a way of making me come apart, in every sense.

He makes sure I have a minute to breathe as he resumes placing soft kisses to my inner thigh. Not wanting to wait any longer, I grab his shoulders in an attempt to pull him up toward me. Despite the intense orgasm I just had, something within me still needs more, and I know it's an emptiness only Lucas can fill. I want to feel him in and around me. I want to be completely consumed by him. I feel bad that I must seem so frantic when he's been nothing but slow and gentle with me tonight, but I'm afraid if I don't hold on now everything that's happened between us will float away and disappear as if it never happened.

"Please, Luc, I need you," I whisper before kissing him hard and deep.

He must sense my desperation, because he reaches up to cup my cheek and kisses me right back before saying "I'm here, babe."

The next thing I know Lucas is covered and pushing inside me, and I know I've never felt more whole in my entire life.

CHAPTER

sixteen

Lucas

BEING WITH KINSLEY TONIGHT IS different. I've never had such a strong desire to go slow and take my time to worship anybody. As corny and bullshit as it might sound, she's my fucking dream girl. Hell, just having her in my bed is a fantasy come to life. Ever since I laid eyes on her half naked body . . . well let's just say she's starred in a lot of morning . . . *ahem* . . . solo performances.

Now, as she lays beneath me, both of us riding out this intense feeling, it's much better having her here in person. I came close to admitting how much I care about her tonight, but I'm glad she stopped me. This is all new—for both of us—and I don't want to risk losing the few parts of her she has actually shared. I get the sense she's trying, but still isn't ready. I don't know what happened to make her so guarded, but it must have been something majorly fucked up. If she is starting to trust me a little more now, even just as a friend, I don't want to screw it up by changing the terms of our deal.

I'm still buried inside her, and have no desire to ever move from this very spot. But then I feel bad I might be crushing her, so I give her a soft kiss on her forehead and reluctantly pull away to lie on my back.

We both relax before she rolls over to curl up next to my side. Her head rests on my chest as her fingers lazily draw patterns against my ribcage. And damn it if my dick doesn't start to stir to life again.

Calm down, boy.

"So, was it good for you?" she breathes, still tracing my skin.

I can't help but chuckle, remembering what I lamely asked her after our first time together at the office party. Thank God we still seem to be us. "Eh, it was all right," I tease back.

She gives me a playful shove and I wrap my arms tighter, pulling her so close that she's half draped on top of me. She curls her left leg around my right and I kiss her hair. I breathe her in—she smells like flowers and cotton candy and it's my new favorite thing to smell in the entire world. I rub my hands up and down her back, and as I glance down I notice some black script scrawled across her left shoulder. I move to sit up so I can get a better look and position her to sit between my legs, her back to my front.

I run my fingers along the dark colored words that contrast so perfectly on her pale skin. *The soul that sees beauty must sometimes walk alone* is scrawled in a delicate, simple script.

"I got that the week my parents died. I guess I was trying to deal with everything and needed a permanent reminder of this." I can tell by the way she stiffens in my arms and keeps staring at the same spot in her lap that she is getting lost in her own faraway thoughts. She tries to put on a brave face and loves to tease and be playful, but I know it's just the way she copes with things. Hell, I do the same thing. She thinks she's able to hide her true feelings, but somehow I'm learning to see through to the real Kinsley. It only fuels my need to protect her and make her feel safe. I know what it's like to lose a parent, but I can't imagine how much tougher it was for her to have both of hers unexpectedly ripped away all at once.

I also know there is still more to her story than she is willing to share with me yet.

But I understand what it means to numb yourself, if only to try and feel something again, as twisted as that logic sounds. I did the same fucking thing and got my own tattoo when things got particularly bad after I ended it with Chelsea.

"You have one, too, right?" Kinsley asks, as if reading my mind. "Did you get it for your mom?"

She scoots to face me and starts scanning my right side. I lean back and prop myself up on my elbows so she can see it as I shrug. It's a picture of an anchor, but the top is crumbling away to reveal a pair of angel wings breaking through and starting to soar upwards. Entwined around the anchor are the words *The struggle is part of the story*. Kinsley inspects it closely before looking gently up at me and whispering "Did it hurt?"

Not knowing exactly what she's referring to, the tattoo or losing my mom, I respond truthfully either way with "Yeah, it hurt like hell." Not wanting her to look so sad, though, I follow up with "But luckily I survived." I lean in to give her a quick kiss on the lips. As much as I love getting to know the deeper parts of Kinsley, it's been an emotional night and I want to see her happy again, not haunted. "Hungry? You didn't eat much at dinner."

"Maybe a little." She admits.

"Good." I stand up and start to walk toward the kitchen.

"Where are you going?" I hear her giggle, still perched on

the bed.

"I wasn't kidding when I said I make a mean grilled cheese. Just you wait—I promise you'll be impressed." I walk to the kitchen and begin to rifle through the fridge to gather up my ingredients.

"And do you always cook naked?" Kinsley trails behind me and leans against the wall at the end of the hallway. She's still naked, too, by the way.

I stand tall, holding cheese in one hand and a loaf of bread in the other, giving her a full frontal view. I feign a shocked expression. "And risk getting burned by hot cheese or some shit? Of course not." I plaster on a big grin and motion to a scrap of fabric hanging on a nearby hook. "I wear an apron, of course."

The sweetest laughter erupts from her lips. I'd do anything to hear her make that sound forever. "But we have to eat it naked. Tastes better that way." I wink at her and she continues to laugh. I'm pretty sure I hear her mumble "You're crazy" as she turns and makes her way back to the bedroom.

"And you love it," I call out loudly as I focus back on the task at hand.

"MMMMOMHYGOODNESSTHISISSOOOGOOD."

"Told you you'd be impressed."

I set up an impromptu picnic on the bed and Kinsley chews her first bite of the grilled cheese I made her. She smiles in between bites and I scarf my own down right beside her.

I hear my phone beep from my pants pocket, still on the floor, so I reach down to pick it up. I see two missed calls from the DSGN offices. It's late on a Friday, so this can't be good. I look from my phone back to Kinsley, who looks completely content laying back, eating a grilled cheese sandwich naked on my bed. In theory this shouldn't be sexy, but it is. I'm just about to toss my phone and the food aside to ravage her all over when my phone beeps again. *Damn it.*

I grudgingly pick up the call with a frustrated "Yeah?"

"Lucas? Hey, it's Chelsea. I'm so sorry to keep calling you on a Friday night, but I'm here at the office working late and I think I screwed up. Erik asked me to back up some new files for the new site and I think I accidentally erased them. I really, really hope I didn't lose them for good, so I don't want to stress him out even more if I don't have to. I thought since you also know this system inside and out, you might be able to help? If you're not busy, that is . . ."

Shit. I run my hand through my hair and rub the side of my face as I contemplate the situation. I really, *really* don't want to leave Kinsley, but if DSGN can't launch next week as planned we will have a big problem.

"Give me ten minutes." I don't bother with a goodbye as I hang up. I get up and start to put my clothes back on. "I'm so sorry Kins . . . I have to run to the office. Chelsea thinks she might have screwed up some important files so I have to go see if I can sort it out."

Kinsley looks confused. "Wait, Chelsea . . . like your ex-girlfriend Chelsea?"

Did I forget to mention she works for Erik? I nod. "She's actually Erik's assistant at DSGN."

She looks dazed before a realization must dawn on her. "Is she the tall blonde you were talking to at the bar?"

"Yeah, that must have been her. Why, did you meet her?" I pull my shirt over my head and zip up my pants.

Kinsley shakes her head and looks as if she might be sick for a second. I hope there wasn't something wrong with the food . . .

But then she takes a deep breath and also gets up to begin

searching for her own clothes. "I'll get my stuff and you can drop me at my place . . ."

I pause to place my hands on her shoulders. "No, please stay here. I'll be as quick as I can."

She looks as if she's having an internal debate before conceding. "You're sure you want me here?"

"There is no place I'd rather have you. In and out, I promise."

I give her shoulder a light squeeze and grab my keys as I rush out the door.

The sooner I go and get this over with, the sooner I can be back home with Kinsley.

Home.

As I practically jog to my car, I realize that this is the first time ever I've thought of my apartment as a real home, and it has everything to do with the girl currently half naked inside it. Home was always the house I lived in with my mom and my dad, but Kinsley makes me start to want things I didn't think I was capable of.

And that thought both comforts and scares the shit out of me.

I PULL UP TO THE DSGN offices, park my car in the garage, and head to the elevators. As I arrive to the twenty-sixth floor and the doors ding open, I notice it's extremely dark and quiet. Not that I expect a full staff, but it's almost eerie.

I walk down the hall and see a light coming from Erik's office. I make my way to the door and push it open. Chelsea is sitting behind Erik's desk. She looks extremely relieved to see me.

"Lucas, thank goodness you're here! I think I really screwed up." She looks down at the floor, obviously embarrassed.

I walk around the side of the desk so I can see the computer screen. It sure seems like the files were wiped all right. Chelsea looks like she's about to cry. "Hey, it's all right." I squeeze her shoulder. "I think I can fix it."

I load up the external hard drive, which does an automatic backup of all the systems every day. After clicking around a bit, I find the most recent backup, and wait for it to load in the system.

Chelsea looks at the screen as the progress bar moves slowly to the right. "Oh my God, Luc, you're the best!" She jumps up and wraps me in a tight hug. I give her a platonic hug back, and I can't help but notice how much different it feels to have Kinsley in my arms.

We release each other and Chelsea takes a step back. I look at the girl in front of me—a girl who I spent five entire years with—and realize I know nothing about her. Nothing that matters, anyway. I have no idea how to really read what she's thinking or how she's feeling. In the short time I've known Kinsley, I feel like I just *get* her. I may not know many factual details about who she is—where she grew up or her first pet's name or how old she was when she learned to ride a bike—but I *know* her. I know her soul. She may be kind of crazy, especially when it comes to love, but then again, so am I.

I've always used Chelsea as a reference point to compare every woman, but that's not fair—nor is it accurate. What Chelsea and I had was what Chelsea and I had. What I feel with Kinsley is something completely different. It might be confusing as hell, but it's us.

I look back at Chelsea and smile, because I finally know it's time to let her go. She stares back at me expectantly.

I put my hands in my pockets and take a step back. "You know, Chels, I just wanted to say I'm sorry. I want you to know what happened between us wasn't your fault. I didn't know who I was or what I needed, but I want to thank you for always being there for me."

The computer makes a beeping noise, indicating the download is ready. It's enough of a distraction to make me realize this isn't the time nor the place for a full, heartfelt conversation. That will come later, but for now I need to get back to Kinsley.

I motion to the computer. "This should be all set now, just double click the file and wait for it to load."

I head for the door when Chelsea calls my name. "Wait, Luc. Are you OK? Did something happen? You seem . . . I don't know. Different."

I think of all the ways Kinsley has helped change me. "Yeah, I feel different. I really think I've changed. For the better. Now it's time to step up and be the man I always hoped I could be." I smile, remembering the way Kinsley's entire face lights up when I make her laugh. Suddenly I can't stand being away from her for another second. "Don't worry, I'll tell you all about it soon."

And with that I rush out of the office, ready to head home to the crazy, beautiful girl waiting for me.

CHAPTER

seventeen

Kinsley

I STAND ALONE IN LUCAS' bedroom after he leaves for the office. I know he said they were still friends, but I didn't realize Chelsea and him basically work together. I completely understand his job being important to him, but I might be just a little jealous he went running as soon as she called. I thought we'd have more time, but maybe he's already realized he's ready for a real relationship again. That he can play the hero to some special somebody who needs him—and whom he needs right back. Something definitely seemed more . . . intimate? passionate? . . . with us tonight, and since he knows I'm not a forever kind of girl, he might want to give things with Chelsea another shot.

This is why I don't do serious. This is why I put up walls. This feeling of getting too close only to have it ripped away is like a glass of ice water to the face. Familiar, painful memories start to creep in, and that's all it takes for the same anger and confusion to take root again.

I know it's my own fault and, given my past experiences, I just can't shake the feeling that I've suddenly gotten in way over my head. Being alone is better. Easier. Isn't it?

I knew it was dangerous to open myself up, even a little bit. Sometimes all it takes is one crack for an entire building to crumble. I'm stuck in a self-destructive spiral that makes me want to scream.

I don't want this.

I can't want this.

But in such a short time—especially after tonight—I've grown so attached to Luc that I'm not sure I have the strength to walk away. He's so sweet and funny and caring and he's slowly working his way into my heart. I know it's crazy, but I'm willing to take whatever he'll give me for now, even if it means sharing him. I want so desperately to believe that I make a difference for him . . . that he can be different for me, too.

I pull my dress over my head and curl up on the edge of Lucas' bed. As my eyes drift closed, I uselessly let myself imagine a life beyond being just friends with Luc. We both have pasts, but maybe our future together can help fade that.

If anyone is going to piece me back together and make me feel whole again, it's Lucas.

Which means he also has the potential to seriously shatter me.

CHAPTER

eighteen

Lucas

THE NEXT MORNING I WAKE up to the smell of bacon, eggs, and pancakes wafting from the kitchen. It takes me a second to fully get my bearings and I realize I'm alone in my bed, still fully clothed from yesterday. When I got home last night, Kinsley was already curled up asleep. She looked so peaceful, so content, that I didn't want to wake her, so I got in bed and passed out myself.

I jump in for a quick shower and throw on a new pair of jeans and white t-shirt before heading into the kitchen. Kinsley is wearing her dress from last night and has her hair pulled up into a messy bun on top of her head. She stands at the stove, scraping the last of some eggs onto a plate. She turns to place it next to the other fully loaded dish at the bar of the island and looks startled when she finally sees me.

"I could get used to this," I say as I make my way to sit on one of the stools.

"It's only fair—you bought dinner and made me a snack last night." She sits beside me and starts to dig into her own plate. "I hope it's OK I raided your fridge."

I load my fork with a big helping of eggs and pancake and shovel it into my mouth. I finish swallowing before responding, "You're welcome to anything in this place to do what you want with, babe." I grab a piece of bacon and give her a cocky wink before devouring it. "Especially me."

She laughs and sips her glass of water. "I'll keep that in mind." She clears her throat and then asks, "So, how did it go last night?"

"Sorry I was gone so long. Chelsea felt really bad about deleting some files so I had to help. It might have screwed up the launch and we can't afford the setback right now."

Kinsley mumbles sarcastically, "Quite the hero, I see."

I tease her back. "You know I'm all about helping a woman in her time of need." I smirk, thinking about how much I loved meeting Kinsley when she tried to fix the sink. The pure joy I felt coming home to find her asleep in my bed only confirmed my deeper feelings. I still need to take things slow so she doesn't shut down on me, but I'm confident this is the right move.

Fuck just being friends. I want more. I'm ready for more.

Speaking of *Moore*, Kinsley looks back at her plate and says more seriously, "I'm glad you were able to help then."

I rest my elbow on the counter and lean toward her. "On Saturdays I usually go to my dad's. He comes home today and I was going to check-in and see how his trip went. Would you like to come with me?"

"I'd love to but I have some work to do. Catch up on some bookkeeping and emails. Raincheck?" She busies herself with clearing her plate, even though she hasn't eaten half of it.

"You got it. I'll drop you off on my way then." I know it's

lame, but I can't stand the thought of not knowing when I'll be able to see her next. I try to think of a way to make plans. "Tomorrow Tristan and Logan are having a party at their beach house. Ryan and I were going to stop by. You should come. Kelley, too."

She doesn't answer right away, but finally agrees. "Sounds good. Text me the details and I'll talk to Kelley. Would you mind if I used your shower first before we leave?" The way she asks so innocently makes me smile.

"Only if I can join you." I give her a smoldering stare.

"I thought you just took a shower?" she shoots back with a matter-of-fact tone.

Thinking quickly, I swipe my finger through the puddle of syrup sitting on my plate and smear it across my cheek. "I seem to have gotten dirty again." I look at her with a not-so-innocent grin.

"Oh, you're dirty all right . . ."

She's just starting to give into her laughter when I reach out and grab her, picking her up in a fireman's hold and heading for the bathroom. I give her a playful slap on the ass and say "Come on babe, I'll show you just how dirty I can really get."

I DROP KINSLEY OFF AT the cottage a few hours later before heading to my dad's house. We would have left earlier, but our sexy shower time turned into sexy get dressed—then undressed and dressed again—time, which also somehow turned into sexy dining room table time.

Like I could say no to any of that?

It's like all of a sudden Kinsley couldn't get enough of me, and I am more than willing to give her everything she wants or needs.

I pull into the drive and see Ryan's truck already parked. He often hangs out on Saturday afternoons with me and my dad. I walk around the back of the house to the garage and see Ry leaning on the picnic table while my dad sorts and unloads fishing gear from the back of his pickup.

"Look who finally decided to show up. I dunno, Luc, I might just be in the lead for favorite son here." Ryan and I often joke about who is my dad's "favorite son." He spent so much time growing up at our house we're practically brothers anyway.

"Fat chance. You're just upset because you miss me."

"Now, now, boys. You know I love ya both the same." My dad comes around the side of the pickup and winks at us before I lean in for a hug.

"Hey, Pop. How was your trip?"

"It was nice. Relaxing. Can't complain. The fish weren't really biting, but it was good all the same." He walks one of his fishing poles into the open garage before going back to the truck for the next. "And what about you? What have you been up to the past few weeks? Did you take care of Kinsley?"

Ryan snorts and I glare at him threateningly. "Yeah, he's taking care of her all right." He doesn't know all of the details about Kinsley and I, but he knows enough to be able to give me crap about it.

My dad looks between Ryan and me before directing a stern, albeit unsurprised, look my way. "Care to fill me in, Lucas?"

I look at my shoes like a five year old who's been caught with his hand in the cookie jar. "She called with a small problem at the cottage so I helped her fix it, just like you asked. Turns out she's cool and we sort of became friends." Both my dad and Ryan stare at me, knowing there's more to the story. "OK, maybe we're a little more than friends. We're sort of . . . friends plus?" I'm close with my dad and all, but this is not exactly something I want him to know all the particulars about.

Ryan smirks. "I knew it. From the first time you talked about her I could tell something was up. Did you finally decide to wake up and stop with the whole 'just friends' thing?"

"Shut up. You're one to talk. When was the last time *you* had a girlfriend?" OK, that's a low blow since I know Ryan's rules about women. He makes sure each girl he's with knows the deal up front: casual flings that only last one night with no chance at something serious. Hell, he's never even let a girl into his apartment. It takes a lot to get to know the guy behind the laid-back smile. He's been through some serious shit, so now he prefers to play it cool. It would take someone very strong and special to break through his defenses.

"And that would be my cue to leave. Well played, bro." Ryan chuckles and shakes his head as he pushes himself off the picnic table. "I've gotta get going anyway. Eli, glad you're back. Luc, we'll talk later." We nod at each other and he makes his way to his truck.

My dad claps Ryan on the shoulder as he passes, then comes to sit on the picnic bench next to me. He stares out into the distance and for a minute I think he's going to change the subject. But then he says, "Start talking, kid," and I know I'm not getting off that easily.

I love my dad but I'm not in the mood for this particular conversation. I'm barely able to get a handle on my own feelings for Kinsley, let alone have anyone else weigh in on the subject.

"What? It's not a big deal. We became close friends and now I'm just trying to see where it goes." I decide it's best not to let him know I've been screwing her silly. Some things are better left unspoken.

"Stop the bullshit, Luc. If you're going to give this a shot with her you better be all in. I know you like to screw around, but I can tell this girl deserves a lot more than some silly casual crap you might try to pull."

It's no use trying to hide it from him. My dad, much like Ryan, can always see straight through me. "I would never hurt Kinsley, Dad. Yeah, I haven't exactly been the best at any sort of real relationship with a girl, but she's different. She's smart, funny, and she makes me want things I didn't even know I wanted. But we both agreed to keep it casual. I really don't want to fuck this up but I don't have a clue what I'm doing. Hell, she's too good for me. I don't deserve her, but she makes me want to be a better man and at least try."

"Listen, kid, I'm not going to tell you what to do because that's for you to figure out. But if I can give you one piece of advice, it's that life is short so there's no use wasting it. If you found a girl who makes you happy—who makes you better—well then you hold onto her and let her know every single day just how much she means to you. I knew that girl was special the minute I met her. She reminds me a lot of your mother, which is why I rented her the cottage." He gets a wistful look on his face, as if recalling a particular memory.

"It's all happened so fast. We've only known each other a short time and I don't want to scare her off by getting too serious."

My dad starts to chuckle at that.

Great—here I am pouring my heart out and he's frigging laughing.

"Luc, did I ever tell you about when I asked your mom to marry me?"

"No, I don't think so."

He smiles and leans forward, resting his hands on his knees before looking over at me. "I asked her the day I met her."

"And she said yes?"

"Hell no. She told me I was crazy."

I laugh at that, thinking about how Kinsley and I seem to share the same sentiment toward each other.

He continues, "But that was OK. I knew she wasn't ready yet. But from the moment I laid eyes on her I knew she was the one for me, so it was my job to reassure her of that every chance I got. No matter how many times she said no, I kept on asking. She once told me that it was my unwavering persistence that finally won her over. She knew that if I could be so certain and patient about us, she would never have to worry. That our whole relationship would be that way. That she could count on me, and that she could feel safe."

"But how were you so sure?"

"Kid, when you know, you know. Don't overthink it." He nudges me in the shoulder and gets up to resume emptying his truck.

I continue to sit for a second, contemplating my dad's words.

When you know, you know.

I think back over the past few weeks, from the first time I heard Kinsley's voice on my phone—hell, to the first time I noticed her at the wedding before I even knew a damn thing about her—to holding her in my arms last night.

I know she's different.

I know I can be myself around her.

I know she really has become my best friend.

. . . and fuck it, I *know* I love her.

CHAPTER

nineteen

Kinsley

IT'S BEEN A FEW HOURS since Lucas dropped me off, and while I'm supposed to be working, I just can't seem to focus.

Waking up in his bed really threw me for a loop. I think it was the best sleep I ever had, and that's not something I should get used to. I made breakfast thinking it would be a last meal of sorts, but just couldn't bring myself to leave. When he invited me to see his dad it took every bit of willpower to decline, but then he invited me to hang out with his friends and seduced me with his dirty shower talk.

And I gave in because he's made me weak. I find myself clinging to any piece of him I can, even if it's only his body. I'm like some sort of junkie and my drug of choice is a brown-haired boy with hazel eyes.

And I really need to quit before I get hooked for good. It's just not as easy as I thought it would be.

A knock at the door just about makes me jump out of my skin. I look at the clock—it's nearly five. For a minute I get disturbingly giddy when I think it might be Lucas, so I rush to answer it.

I pull open the door to find Eli standing on the porch. While not who I was hoping to see, it's really good to see him.

I push open the screen. "Hey, I heard you were back. How was the trip?" I step aside so he can come in.

As he passes through the doorway he says, "It was good, but it's nice to be home." He pauses for a moment when he sees the paintings hanging on the wall. A nostalgic smile lights up his face, and for a minute I think he's going to tear up. But he clears his throat and turns to look back at me. "I wanted to stop by and make sure everything is OK. Lucas said he's been keeping an eye on you, but I had to see for myself."

I feel myself blush, hoping Lucas didn't tell his dad too many details about our newly formed *friendship*. "He's definitely been a huge help." I put a little too much emphasis on the word *huge*.

Crap. Jeez, Kins, why not tell him all the dirty details about the past month.

I stand up a little straighter, trying to muster some level of indifference and control. "As you can see, the place is still standing." I wave my hand around, hoping to redirect his attention anywhere but on me. I'm sure my face is giving a lot more away than I intend it to these days.

Eli smiles and says, "Well that's good. Glad to hear it."

We stand there in an awkward silence before Eli gathers himself and takes a few steps back toward the door. I find it odd that he came all the way out here just for that, but he pauses before turning back to me.

"You know, Kinsley, I'm really glad to hear you and Lucas are friends now. I can tell you've been a good influence on him."

Eli beams, and I can't help but feel like a fraud.

"Me? I'm not so sure about that. He was doing pretty well on his own, I think." I'm not sure what to say without giving away all the specifics of our time together. I'm sure Lucas is more . . . *satisfied* since meeting me, but that's not something I can explain to his dad for crying out loud.

He shakes his head. "You might not see it, but I do. I'm sure he told you about his mom, right?"

I nod, swallowing thickly. It's one thing to hear Lucas talk about his mom, but hearing Eli talk about the love of his life might be too much for me to take.

"Well Luc has had a bit of a rough time with that, and for a while nobody could get through to him. I've done my best, and so has Ryan, but he hasn't had a lot of female influences in his life." He looks down at his shoes, as if feeling guilty for that. It's not like it's his fault, though.

He takes a deep breath and looks back up at me. "I wanted to come by and say thank you. I know you may not think you did anything particularly special, but I want you to know that I see a change in him. A good one. And for that I will be eternally grateful."

I can't think of anything to say. I can barely move. I can feel those stupid tears prick the backs of my eyes again and I'll be damned if I let them loose on this poor, unsuspecting man.

He finishes by simply stating, "I'm really happy you've been able to help each other out," and with that he smiles and lets himself out.

As soon as the door closes, I give in and allow a couple tears to fall.

CHAPTER

twenty

Lucas

THERE ARE FEW THINGS BETTER than spending a cool afternoon at the beach, nursing a beer and watching Tristan make an ass of himself.

Currently he is trying to convince a pair of blonde twins that he and his brother would be a perfect fit for them—in every sense. Sadly, I think they're buying it. Tristan motions toward Logan and whispers something, and all it takes for the girls to nod enthusiastically at whatever T says is for Logan to flash his dimpled smile.

"Well, kids, looks like I'm needed elsewhere. Don't wait up." Logan winks and grabs another beer on his way over to his brother, leaving Ryan and me to stand by the makeshift bar, which is really just a couple of coolers filled with beer bottles and ice.

Ryan shakes his head. "Why girls fall for that guy, I will never understand. I mean, sure, him and Logan are good looking, but when T opens his mouth they must realize what bullshit comes out of it."

I take a swig of my beer. "I don't think they spend much time talking. From what I hear, more things are going in mouths than coming out."

"Dude, I so did not need that visual." He shuts his eyes as if trying to un-see something.

Ryan is no prude, but he more or less lives by a never kiss and tell policy. Tristan, on the other hand, likes to talk about nothing *but* all the kissing he does. They've always butted heads, but it's mostly in good fun.

After we shoot the shit for a little while, Ryan points out that Kinsley and Kelley are here. I must look like a damn fool with a giant grin plastered across my face when I see Kinsley, but fuck if I care.

They walk over to us and I casually grab Kinsley's belt loop to pull her close to me. "Hey, I'm glad you could come." And then I lean down to whisper so only she can hear me, "And I plan on making you come again tonight."

She blushes in her adorable way and gently pushes me away, but I know she secretly loves it by the way she squeezes my arm a second later. We're by no means exclusive—yet—but I'll take any small victory I can get.

Then we see Tristan and Logan openly making out with the two girls from earlier. "Jeez you guys, get a room." Ryan pretends he's disgusted by their PDA. I can tell he's joking, but that doesn't mean I won't still give him a hard time about it.

"Hey, man, you're just jealous." I tilt my beer toward him. "Someday you'll know what it's like to be in love just like they are."

He snickers. "Yeah, I wouldn't hold your breath on that my friend."

"Quite the optimist, aren't you?" Kelley chimes in.

Ryan looks at her without missing a beat. "Just a realist. I don't like to set up unrealistic expectations. In business *or* my personal life." He shrugs as if it's just true facts.

This is usually where girls will get all doe-eyed as if Ryan is simply some poor, misguided bastard they can change, but Kelley actually looks like she agrees.

"I think that's smart."

"Gee, Ry. Maybe you've finally met the female version of yourself." I nod toward Kelley, who looks just as easy-going as Ryan usually is. They even have the same shade of dark brown hair, although hers is long and straight compared to his short, messy mop.

Ryan studies her for a minute, almost sizing her up, before asking, "And I'm supposed to believe you aren't looking for true love or anything, right?"

"Oh, no, I am. I just also happen to think there's no sense in wasting anyone's time if you know it isn't going to go anywhere."

If I didn't know better, I'd say Ryan looks caught off guard, but he calmly raises his bottle of water and says, "I'll drink to that." He leans down to grab a bottle of beer and hands it to Kelley.

He motions toward Kinsley to ask if she wants one, but she politely declines.

"I'm going to go grab my phone from the car. I'm expecting an important message from a client."

"I tried to tell her even God took a day to rest, but she wouldn't listen to me." Kelley holds her arms up and shrugs as if she's not responsible.

Kinsley's face lights up playfully. "Clearly he never ran his own business." She takes a few steps back before adding, "I'll be quick, promise." She turns to make her way toward the driveway and I take the opportunity to admire the rear view.

Ryan laughs, "I think you're actually drooling."

I give his arm a light shove. I subtly wipe my chin, though. Just in case. That only makes him laugh harder.

Kelley takes a sip from her bottle before turning toward me. "So, Lucas, that was a pretty great party for DSGN the other week. I'm glad things worked out . . . with the office and everything."

"Yeah, you guys were a big help. Thanks again. The launch went well and we even have a couple of big media companies sniffing around. It's only a matter of time before they hit it big."

"It's great that these startups can trust you to take care of them."

"I try." I take a drink and look out at the water.

"I bet they're often scared of taking that next big step, but you're there to help them take it slow, knowing you're working in their best interests." She looks straight at me with serious eyes. Not threatening exactly, but suddenly I sense we're not really talking about my business.

I proceed cautiously. "I do my best to make it as easy as possible for them, but ultimately they have to take the leap themselves."

"But you would never intentionally mislead them, right?"

Realizing her true meaning, I match her stare, not backing down. "I always do what's best for them. I live, sleep, eat, and breathe thinking of them. I would never let anything bad happen, let alone hurt them."

Ryan looks at me, then back at Kelley, then back to me like some sort of confused bobble head.

Kelley's intense gaze finally relaxes. "Then they're lucky to have you."

"I'm the lucky one."

Ryan chuckles and shakes his head, as if amused by Kelley's passive aggressive interrogation.

By her pleased expression, I'd say I passed.

Kinsley finally returns, completely unaware of what just happened. "Sorry. Did ya miss me?"

"I sure as hell did." Ryan interjects dryly before I have a chance to respond. Now I know he's just egging me on.

"Don't mind him. He's just cranky because you get all my attention lately." I pat Ryan's shoulder. "But don't worry, bro. You're still my main bitch."

"Sorry, Luc, you know I won't play second string for anyone. Time to go find me a new piece of ass." He finishes his water with one final swig and moves to head toward the house.

Not wanting him to get the final jab I call out, "Oh, come on, we can work it out!" to which his response is a simple extension of his middle finger above his head without even looking back.

Kelley, Kinsley, and I are left behind to laugh our asses off.

CHAPTER

twenty-one

Kinsley

"WHAT ABOUT THIS?" KELLEY HOLDS up a hot pink lycra mini dress and waggles it on the hanger in front of me.

I snatch it away from her and hold it up to my body. It looks like it would barely cover my ass . . . or my boobs. "Yeah, I'm sure this is the perfect choice for a fancy work dinner." I giggle while rolling my eyes and hang the blindingly bright fabric back on the rack it came from.

"We've been at this mall for hours and so far everything is either too casual or too fancy or too slutty. You gotta pick out something, Goldilocks, or you're going to end up going to this thing naked." She stops shuffling through another clothing rack to wiggle her eyebrows at me. "Although I'm sure Lucas wouldn't mind that."

"At least that would cut down on my getting ready time." I shrug as Kell gives me an intrigued look. I roll my eyes. "Kidding.

I'm just very . . . particular. You know that. Lucas said this was an important dinner with the people from DSGN and some other impressive company that wants to buy them or something. I want to make sure I make a good impression and don't make a fool of myself."

Kelley stops rifling through the rack and rests her hands on top. "And you don't find it odd that he asked you to go?"

I shrug and continue flipping through hangers filled with assorted tulle and chiffon. "No. He asked me, as his friend, so he wouldn't have to go alone. No big deal."

She eyes me suspiciously. *"Riight."*

"What?"

She stands up straight and focuses back on the clothes. "Nothing. I just find it interesting is all."

I let my curiosity get the better of me. "Interesting how?"

She looks back at me. "Just from my experience, a casual fuck buddy is not someone that gets invited to important work dinners. They might be on the late night snack menu, but they're certainly not appropriate for the main course. Catch my drift?"

I stare back at her, trying not to give myself away. "I mean it, Kell. It's not like that. Yes, we might be *fuck buddies*, as you so eloquently put it, but we're also friends. We can hold an actual conversation, so tonight is nothing special. Not for us, anyway." I move down another aisle, pretending to find something I like.

Truth is, I'm nervous as all hell. I haven't seen much of Lucas since last week and we haven't had any alone time. We were both catching up on work, and since GS Ventures launched the DSGN site and this big potential deal happened, Luc has been really busy fielding calls and going over numbers and spreadsheets. He called last night and asked me to come to dinner, and while I'm afraid I'll do or say something completely ridiculous being around all these smart business types (let alone just by being around *him*), I don't want to disappoint Lucas . . . or his dad. Ever since I talked to Eli, I feel like they're both counting on me.

Plus, I don't want to miss another opportunity to see Lucas looking all sorts of delicious in a suit. I've missed being around him, and so have my lady parts.

I continue to make my way around the racks and racks of dresses, waiting for something to jump out at me. I want to look and feel confident. I round the corner of one of the aisles, when suddenly I see it: the most perfect dress. It's a simple yet elegant deep lavender chiffon gown that hugs tight at the top and flows down to mid-calf, with light gold beaded straps crisscrossing against the back.

Kelley must simultaneously notice the beautiful garment draped on the center mannequin, because she walks right over to stand next to it. She looks once at the dress, then once at me before crossing her arms and saying matter-of-factly, "If this isn't the one, then you really are going to have to go naked."

CHAPTER

twenty-two

Lucas

HOT. DAMN.

I can barely pick my jaw up off the floor as Kinsley stands in her doorway looking more amazing than I ever thought possible. She's wearing some type of purple dress that is hugging her in all the right places and these sexy, strappy heels that I'd like to see her in nothing but. Visions of her bent over her kitchen counter wearing just the heels as I pound into her from behind flash through my mind.

What? It's been a long week . . .

Seriously, she's beautiful. Fully clothed and all. I mean this girl looks incredible in baggy jeans and no makeup, but tonight she's fucking radiant. I realize for the first time I can't wait to go out with a girl. With *this* girl.

And after dinner, finally tell her I love her. It's not going to be easy, but I like a challenge.

I figure if I can make my living risking millions of dollars on people I barely know, then I sure as shit can risk my heart if it means I get to be with Kinsley—as more than just a friend.

"Wow. You're killing me, Kins," seem to be the only words I can get to move from my mind to my mouth.

"You're not so bad yourself, there, handsome." The way she beams at me with genuine happiness thankfully makes my brain start to function properly. "Ready for tonight?"

Her smile clouds with a hint of concern and I can tell she's nervous. I'll have to do my best to keep her at ease. I know it's going to be a stuffy, tense business thing, but I don't want Kinsley to feel like she can't be herself. It might not be an ideal night, but I really want her to be with me.

"If by ready you mean ready for dinner to be over so I can bring you home and do all sorts of dirty things to you, then yes, I am so fucking ready." I move closer to grab her hips and kiss her long and hard.

She relaxes as she melts into me. She then pulls back and grins devilishly before grabbing my arm and pulling me toward the front porch steps. "Then let's go and do this thing."

It's going to be torture trying to keep my hands off her through dinner. Thankfully Logan is going to handle most of the negotiations. I prefer the more technical side of things, whereas he's all about the charm and the show. It's going to be a long night, but it at least boosts my ego to know Kinsley's just as impatient as me.

WE ARRIVE AT *LUXE*, THE fanciest, most expensive restaurant in town, a few minutes later. I'm typically not into the whole wine and dine bullshit, but I've learned it's part of the job. Rich guys like Jack Parker and Theo Peterman—of Parker + Peterman

Industries, the largest tech company on the East Coast—spend obscene amounts of money like it's nothing. I'm not going to pretend I, myself, am not well off, but I work hard for every penny I earn. And while I may have been immature in the past, now I know better than to make a big deal out of it or try to flaunt it. For these guys, though, it's like the price of our meal directly correlates to how important we are or some shit. It's all just a big pissing contest. They try to schmooze us so we'll sell them DSGN, and we try to impress them enough to buy it. It'd be much faster and easier to just whip our dicks out and measure.

I toss my keys to the valet and spread my hand against the small of Kinsley's back in a possessive gesture as I lead her toward the door. I noticed the way he let his eyes feast on her when she stepped out of the car, and I'll be damned if I let anyone think she isn't already taken.

As I feel the silkiness of her dress and the slightest hint of her skin beneath my fingers, I realize I'm not going to be able to control myself through dinner. I've waited all week for this woman, important meeting be damned.

We enter through the heavy front door and I quickly scan the entryway. Before she has a chance to react, I grab Kinsley's arm and quickly lead her down the side hallway I know leads to the restrooms. She starts to say something, but I'm ducking us both into the closest women's bathroom—which, thankfully, is unoccupied—and have her back up against the door within a few seconds flat. This woman drives me to do some crazy things, but I love that it's her. No apologies, no regrets.

I click the lock closed and push myself against Kinsley's body. She obviously gets where this is going, because she drops her purse and just as excitedly clings to me before our lips meet in a rough kiss. Our hands and mouths are everywhere at once, neither of us able to get enough. Her fingers move to my waist as she expertly has my belt unhooked, button undone, zipper un-zipped, and pants pushed halfway down my legs in an elegantly choreographed manner.

I go to reach my hands under her dress, but the next thing I know she's taking control by pushing me backward. I let her lead me, our lips still joined, over to a small couch—*Wait, they get fucking couches in here?*—where she shoves me down to a sitting position and kneels before me.

She grabs my cock in one hand and pumps up and down a few times before I feel her perfect mouth encompass me. I tangle my hands in her hair as she continues to bob up and down with the perfect pressure from her delicate hand and the best sucking sensation coming from her incredible lips. I already know she's an amazing kisser, but it seems like she is amazing at all things concerning her mouth, flirty banter and blowjobs included.

I feel like a horny teenager with how fast I could probably come, but I want that to happen buried within my gorgeous girl. I desperately pant, "I need to be inside you, babe," before she has mercy on me and eases off. I grab a condom from my wallet as she stands up and moves to straddle me. I help her gather her dress around her hips, easing myself deep inside her.

She isn't wearing any underwear and I just about blow my load yet again.

She must read the realization on my face because she leans in to whisper "I knew they would be wet all night, and I told you I hate wearing wet underwear."

I grin and grab her ass tighter as she rides me faster and harder, letting out these insanely sexy moans. It's then we hear a knock at the door, to which Kinsley breathlessly calls out "Mmmbusy!"

I wrap my arms around her back to pull her as close as I can—which still isn't close enough—and bury my face in her neck. "Come with me, Kins," I whisper, and we both explode with a final, hard thrust.

I continue to hold her close to me for a beat, feeling her inhale and exhale as she holds onto my neck.

Goddamn she feels so perfect, so right, here in my arms.

I gently push her hair back from her face and run my hand down her cheek. "Ready for dinner now?"

She laughs and nods as I stand us both up, gently lowering her to her feet. She smooths her dress back over her legs and touches up her lip gloss in the mirror as I pull my pants back up and secure them around my waist. She unlocks the door and goes to open it before I put my hand up to stop it.

I lean down close to her ear and whisper, "And that's just a preview of tonight," before sliding my arm away and allowing us to walk out, gaining an open-mouthed stare from an elderly woman waiting outside.

I wink at the flabbergasted woman as we walk past, leading Kinsley back to the front of the restaurant. As I give the maître d' my name and wait for him to lead us to our table, Kinsley runs her fingers down my arm before settling her hand in mine. I never knew holding a girl's hand could be so . . . intimate. Well, holding *Kinsley's* hand is anyway. I give her palm a gentle squeeze, assuring both of us that we're in this together.

The maître d' motions for us to follow him and we make our way to the back of the restaurant to a private, secluded table. As we approach, I see Logan, Erik, Jack, and Theo already talking amongst themselves. Then I notice a fifth person at the end of the table. I didn't know Chelsea would be here tonight, but from the look of her revealing attire and the way Jack's eyes keep slipping toward her overexposed cleavage, I can guess why Erik brought her along. I nod to Logan and Erik as they each stand up to greet me, and I am just about to introduce Kinsley to the table when Chelsea narrows her eyes toward the pretty girl next to me.

"And who's this, Lucas?" she says, genuinely curious.

"This is Kinsley, my uh, friend." I didn't really think about how to introduce her, but she seems comfortable enough as I then introduce everyone at the table. I don't miss how Kinsley blushes when she hears Erik's name. I give her a knowing grin as if to say *Yup, it was his desk* as I move to pull out her chair and take my own seat to her right.

We all peruse the menu and make small talk before ordering.

"So, Kinsley, what is it you do?" Theo Peterman fixes his eyes on Kinsley and leans toward her.

"Nothing quite as interesting as all of you, I suppose, but I design floral arrangements."

I hate to hear her try to sell herself short. It's no easy task starting and running a small business. We all have to start somewhere, and it takes guts to even take that first step. "Don't let her modesty fool you. She runs a very successful business and does it all on her own. I have to say it's pretty impressive to watch her work." I keep my eyes trained on Kinsley. I mean what I say. This girl impresses the shit out of me. When I think back to having my dad and Logan and Ryan there to launch GS Ventures, I can't imagine doing it by myself. My dad was our first investor, so from the very start we had a generous financial backing and were able to delegate tasks out to others. I've gathered enough info from our conversations together to know Kinsley built her business literally from nothing, and did it herself. It's seeing dedicated people like her that reminds me why I wanted to invest in companies in the first place—to help turn passionate ideas into real, profitable businesses.

"I always like to see someone with that genuine entrepreneurial spirit. Not everyone is cut out for it, but the way I see it, running a business is running a business, big or small. Hell, the small business owners I meet tend to work ten times harder than most of the wealthy CEOs I know. Good for you, darlin'." Theo raises his glass of whiskey toward Kinsley before taking a long swig and turning back to Erik to talk shop.

I cast a sideways glance at Kinsley and squeeze her knee under the table. I leave my hand resting there for a few seconds, before letting it slowly glide further and further up her thigh. I feel her react subtly, but she's trying to act as if it's not affecting her. Erik and Logan include me in their conversation with Jack and Theo, looking for me to confirm some facts and figures while Logan handles the real sell. I continue to let my fingers explore Kinsley's upper thighs, feeling pretty smug, when suddenly I feel a gentle hand cup my balls.

I chance a quick peek at Kinsley's face, but she pretends to be interested in the boring conversation about turnover rates and target markets.

I thought our quickie would have taken the edge off but, according to my dick, apparently not.

I try to focus my energy on the conversation happening between the four men beside me. A. It will hopefully be a distraction so I won't throw Kinsley down and have her right here during dinner, and B. Maybe if I help Logan out a bit more we can close this deal faster and get home to an encore presentation of what Kinsley and I started in the bathroom.

CHAPTER

twenty-three

Kinsley

Lucas amazes me with how smart he is about business and numbers. I knew he had to be smart to do what he does but I've never really seen him in action before.

Turns out it's a major turn-on. Listening to him confidently talk about financial forecasts and streams of revenue is downright mesmerizing. I drown out everyone and everything around me to focus solely on him. For a minute I even forget about the blonde sitting across from me. Why does she have to be so pretty? And she seems genuinely nice, which makes it even worse.

Ooh, a strong hand on my thigh is a nice distraction . . .

As Lucas' hand slides further and further up my leg I can't help but grab him right back. It's not fair that only one of us should suffer with want. He needs to know he can't get to me, that I can handle him.

Except this plan sort of backfires, because as soon as I feel him start to get hard again, I only get wetter. And he's doing a really good job of pretending we're not groping each other under the table as he talks about the potential of DSGN.

I can only take so much, and just as his fingers graze dangerously close to my girly bits, I decide it's probably best for me to excuse myself to the bathroom. It's either that or let him finger me with an audience. I'm willing to be pretty adventurous—especially when it comes to Luc—but even that might be crossing the line during a business dinner. I grasp his hand—just in time—and drop it back in his own lap as I clear my throat and quietly excuse myself. He grins at me devilishly, knowing the exact effect he's having on me. *Sexy bastard.*

I make my way to the familiar hallway, recalling the particulars of my last trip this way.

There is a small line outside the door so I lean back against the wall trying not to spontaneously combust from all my recent pent up sexual frustration. I'm not sure I've ever been so turned on, despite having that amazing orgasm less than an hour ago—it's as if I didn't just suck and ride Lucas like an insane, depraved sex-addict in the very bathroom I'm now waiting to use. I was going to behave until after dinner, but Luc clearly had other plans. I wasn't expecting him to pull me into the bathroom, or for me to need him so badly. Taking control is the only way I could think to get through tonight. The plan is to show him I know what I want—and am not afraid to take it—in the hopes that he trusts I know what I'm doing.

But the thing is, I'm not sure I do know exactly what I want, or how to get it for that matter. I think I've underestimated just how much I've come to depend on Luc, and I can't help but wonder if we might have a chance at something real. I want so badly to believe in a future I never thought could exist for me, but I'm too certain—and terrified—it will all just blow up in my face.

I sense someone right behind me, so I glance over my shoulder. *Chelsea. Grreeat.*

"Kinsley, right?" The blonde tilts her head and looks at me as if she really doesn't remember my name.

"Yup, that's me."

"So how long have you and Lucas been . . . *friends?*" She spits that last word as if it's leaving a bad taste in her mouth.

"I don't know. A couple of months maybe?" I mentally kick myself for how lame that sounds. I was going for laid-back, but I think it reads more as defensive.

She leans against the wall next to me. "I just hope you know what you're doing. Lucas isn't really the type to settle down, if you know what I mean." I don't know if she's genuinely trying to look out for me or if she's just being catty, but I decide to play nice.

"Yeah, I know. I'm not either. Seriously, we're just friends. I think he might be ready for more of a relationship with someone soon, though, but trust me, it's not with me." The more I say it out loud, maybe the more it will be true. It's almost comical that I actually thought for a second I stood a chance.

Chelsea looks relieved, as if I've just dismissed her worst fear. "Really? You think so? Because I thought he seemed different the other night when he came to help me. I couldn't tell what he was getting at, but he said he would tell me soon. Now it might make perfect sense."

The way she looks so hopeful makes me feel sick. I think to myself, *Yeah, he just needs to find a way to remove his current emotionally unavailable albatross—me.*

Of course he would choose to be with someone like Chelsea. She's more than capable of giving him the love that he needs. I really have no reason to be upset . . . I don't think I can give him what she is clearly ready for.

But for the first time in a long time I wish more than anything I could.

I force a smile. "I hope it works out."

Thankfully the bathroom becomes available, so I use my last ounce of composure to shuffle into the bathroom before clutching the sink as I try to get enough air to fill my lungs. I thought I was ready to open up and let someone into my soul . . . even as a friend. But this is just another reminder that it's less painful to keep them shut out. Completely. If I only have to rely on myself, I can't get hurt. I should know better by now.

I look up to stare at my reflection in the mirror. From the corner of my eye I can see the couch Lucas and I christened earlier. Now all I can think of is Chelsea and him on it, sharing the same passion and need for each other, and the thought makes my heart constrict.

As confused and hurt as I feel, though, this is still a big night for Lucas, Logan, and Erik so I won't cause a scene. I look to the mirror to give myself a pep talk. "Pull it together, Kins. Just get through the rest of dinner and then you can fall apart. Stick to the plan, end this before you act any crazier, and then you can go back to your normal, isolated life."

I take a deep breath and head back toward the table, not even daring to glance at Chelsea as I quickly make my way past.

I SLIDE INTO MY SEAT and avoid making eye contact with Lucas as much as possible. As if he can sense the change in my demeanor, he gently squeezes my knee and forces me to look at him. I plaster on the biggest, fakest smile I can muster and then busy myself with the food that has arrived in front of me. Lucas acknowledges me with his own half-smile, although I can tell he looks concerned. Erik then starts asking Luc about some figure for their estimated revenue, which thankfully draws his attention away from me. Things seem to be going well and as bad as I feel, I would never want to ruin this meeting for them.

Chelsea returns to her own seat a moment later and smiles at me as if we're new best friends. The fact that I could ever have let myself believe I could be the one for Luc is enough to make me lose my dinner.

Thank heavens the negotiations kick into high gear and all the men stay occupied for the remainder of the meal. At some point, Lucas' hand find its way back to my leg, and I let him keep it there, but I don't return the favor this time. I both need and hate his touch right now.

After what feels like forever, Jack stands up and claps Erik on the back. "We certainly have a lot to think about. You boys have a damn fine idea here, and once Theo and I get a chance to talk to the rest of our people, we'll be in touch." Logan and Luc stand to shake hands with Jack and Theo. Both men nod toward me and Chelsea, and Theo mutters a "Good luck" as he passes me to leave. As soon as they are out of earshot, Logan and Erik start high-fiving.

"I'd say that went well. They were impressed." Logan finishes off his glass of scotch before setting it down on the table and relaxing into his chair.

"Man, I feel like celebrating. Who wants to head out for some drinks?" Erik motions to himself. "On me, of course."

Lucas leans back and loosens his tie before glancing over to me and furrowing his brow. "I think we're going to get going, but thanks for the offer."

We both stand and say our goodbyes to the table. Lucas puts his hand on the small of my back to lead me out the door. He gives his ticket to the valet and we stand quietly as his car is driven around. Lucas opens the passenger door for me and I slip inside. He gets in the driver's seat, and eases us out of the parking lot.

The drive to the cottage is short, and the entire ride is spent in complete silence. After Lucas pulls his car into the drive, he shuts off the ignition before turning his head to look at me.

"Kins? Do you want to tell me what happened tonight?" He sounds tired and concerned, his voice soft.

I'm not sure what I want to say, so I try to stall. "What do you mean?"

"I mean I thought we were having a great night, and then you went to use the bathroom and when you came back you seemed different. Upset. Did something happen?"

I fidget with my hands in my lap, trying to focus on some detached distraction enough to clear my head. I need to do this—for both of us—I'm just not sure how to start.

So much for taking charge of the situation.

I'm sure he can feel the air shift in the car as my hands tense and I hold my breath. I look back down to my lap, searching for the right words. I should be happy that Lucas is finally ready to give love a shot, but the fact that it's not with me still tugs at my heart. If I know one thing about Lucas it's that he's loyal. He won't want to let me down by breaking our deal, so I have to be the one to let him go.

"I want you to know I've really enjoyed hanging out with you these past few weeks."

I can see Lucas' Adam's apple bob up and down as he swallows thickly. "What are you getting at, Kins?"

"I think that it's time for us both to move on. We've had our fun and it was great, but we know it's not going anywhere. I told you from the start I wasn't looking for a relationship, so this really shouldn't come as a surprise."

. . . Except our relationship has been nothing but surprising.

He gets really quiet before saying, "So that's it . . . we're done? Just like that?"

I don't enjoy seeing him look so confused. It's as if he can't believe it's going to be that easy. As much as it pains me to have to do this, it's the only way to save us both. I can feel myself falling for this man a little more each minute I spend with him, and I'm afraid it would be my undoing if I were to lose him down the road. I can't trust that I'm enough for him, and I can't guarantee I can fully let him in. Tonight proves that. We both know what it's like to lose those close to us, and from the intensity of our short time together I can tell if anything really bad happened between us, neither of us could recover. Despite everything, I still deeply care for Lucas, and don't want to ever see him hurt. I'm doing this to save us. Better to stop things while we'll only get bruised rather than completely wrecked.

"I think it will be easier for us both to end this now, while things are still good. It was fun while it lasted, but we both knew it would have to end eventually. We can still be friends, just without the benefits . . ."

Seriously? Could I make this sound any more lame? I'm desperately trying to hold onto some part of him, but I know that would just be torture for me. Just give him a clean break, Kins.

He shakes his head and lets out a derisive chuckle before getting serious again. "I can't just be your friend anymore, Kinsley."

Ouch. "OK. I get that." It comes out as barely a whisper. "Thanks for showing me a good time, Luc. I really hope you find someone who deserves you."

And with that I get out of the car, forcing myself to not look back no matter how much I want to—just to look into his intense, hazel eyes one more time. To let him see right into me as if we are the only two people in the world in this moment and neither the past nor the future mean anything.

I unlock the cottage door with shaking hands, and sink to the floor as it closes behind me.

My mouth is dry, my heart aches, and my vision blurs as tears start to stream down my face in silent agony. It's as if someone just punched me in the stomach repeatedly until it hurts so bad I've gone numb again.

So much for just getting bruised.

CHAPTER

twenty-four

Lucas

IT'S BEEN FOUR WEEKS SINCE Kinsley ripped my heart out
and stomped on it, and whoever said that bullshit about time
healing all wounds is a fucking liar. I feel just as shitty today as I
did that night, and have felt this way every single day in between.

And you want to know the really messed up part?

I still fucking love her.

And there isn't a damn thing I can do about it. She wanted
out, and I let her go. That was the deal.

There's a knock at my apartment door but I don't give a
shit. I simply cover my head with one of my pillows. I've been
laying in this bed for the better part of these past few weeks. I
keep smelling Kinsley's hair on the pillows, and it drives me insane. But that doesn't stop me from inhaling as deeply as I possibly can. Nothing else matters or feels worth getting up for. Not
work, not dinner with my dad. I keep making excuses that I have

some sort of bug I can't shake. It's easier than explaining what really happened, and it keeps people away. I know I'm being a complete pussy letting a girl get to me like this, but it's not just any girl. It's Kinsley. *My* girl.

And that's the real kick in the balls. She never really was mine, was she?

I hear a key jiggle in the lock before the door opens and footsteps pound down the hall.

"Dude. You look like shit."

"Thanks, bro. You can leave the same way you came in." My voice comes out muffled from under the pillows. Leave it to Ryan to not show any sympathy.

"So you're still not going to tell me what happened with Kinsley?"

At the sound of her name, I spring into protective mode and turn to sit up on my elbows. "Who said anything happened with her?"

"Come on, Luc. If anybody has the ability to make you completely lose your mind, it's her. You never go off the grid like this. Logan said the deal with DSGN went through and he could barely get ahold of you to sign the papers."

I sigh and fall back against the pillows, squeezing my eyes shut while pinching my thumb and forefinger over the bridge of my nose. "It's nothing. I've just been sick."

"Oh, you're fucking sick all right."

"Shut up." I fling a pillow in his direction.

"That's it, you leave me no choice." I hear him pull something from his pocket and I open my eyes to see him tap the screen on his phone before holding it up to his ear.

"Hey Eli, it's me."

"Seriously? You're calling my dad on me?"

He tilts the phone away from his mouth and smirks. "Hey,

desperate times call for desperate measures."

I roll away from him and mutter a few choice curse words under my breath.

ABOUT TWENTY MINUTES LATER I can hear Ryan leave as he says goodbye to my dad, who must have just gotten here. I hear some clattering in the kitchen so I decide to get up and get this over with. As I make my way down the hall, I can smell coffee brewing as my dad stands by the counter making a pair of sandwiches.

"Ry was right. You look like hell."

"He didn't have to call you. I'm fine, Dad." I slump down onto the barstool and rest my head on my hands.

"Cut the crap, Lucas." He slides a plate with a giant turkey sandwich toward me. My mouth instantly waters—I haven't felt much like eating lately, but by the way my stomach growls I guess it's hungry. "Eat this and then tell me what you did to screw things up with Kinsley."

I take a big bite of the sandwich and then shoot my dad an incredulous look. "What makes you think it was my fault?"

"So this does have to do with her." He grins, knowing I fell right into his trap. *Damn.*

No use trying to lie now. I finish half of the sandwich before setting the rest down on my plate. I take a deep breath, not sure where to begin. "There's not much to tell. She gave up on us. That's it. Game over."

Except I didn't want it to be a game anymore.

I maybe tried to change the rules, but look how well that worked out for me.

"Do you want it to be over?"

"Of course not. I lov—I still care about her."

"And yet you just let her walk away? Who really gave up here?" My dad looks at me with a stern yet sympathetic look.

I let out a frustrated sigh. "What was I supposed to do? She said she doesn't want a relationship and I don't know how to fix that."

"Sounds like you're not really showing her that it's anything worth having, there, kid. How is she supposed to trust you care about her if you won't even try to talk to her, let alone fight for her."

I really hate it when he makes sense.

"I don't want to push her. Maybe she really is better off without me." I think back to the emptiness I saw in Kinsley's eyes as she told me it was just fun. I helped put that look there by not arguing to the contrary, and I've hated myself every second since. I wanted to fight. I wanted to pull her into my arms and never let her go. But she was so distant I didn't want to upset her more. If she doesn't want to be with me . . . well I just want her to be happy. It's not fair for me to assume she's ready for more just because I am. I knew her expectations going in, so what right do I have forcing her into something else?

"Let me tell you something, Luc. That girl is a lot stronger than you're giving her credit for. But she needs you. Anyone can see that. Did it ever occur to you that when she's pulling away, that's when you need to hold on tighter? She's lost more in her short life so far than most should have to deal with, it's no wonder she's scared to let someone in. And I know it's hard for you to let another women into your life since we lost your mother, so I'm not saying it's going to be easy. But you have to ask yourself if she's worth it."

I don't need to think about it. "She's worth everything."

"Good. Now show her that."

He tousles my hair like he used to when I was a kid before

turning to clean up the kitchen.

Now I see what a royal douchebag I've been. Kinsley needs me just as much as I need her, and I have to let her know I won't give up on us ever again—not for anything.

"So how do you think I can show her—Dad?" As I turn back to ask my father for a little more advice, my heart crashes right to my feet as I see him lean over and grab his chest. I rush around the counter to grab him before he falls, but he's dead weight in my arms as he slumps toward the ground, unconscious.

CHAPTER

twenty-five

Kinsley

YOU KNOW THAT FEELING YOU get in the morning—that space between awake and dreaming where you're aware of what's going on, but it all seems hazy?

That's how I've felt for the past month away from Lucas.

I'm conscious, but it all seems fuzzy. I work just to get through the day, and sleep is a sweet escape where I can dream of being back in his warm, safe arms. The past few days have been cloudy and dreary as if even mother nature can feel the brokenness of my heart.

So many times I've picked up my phone to call or text him to tell him some silly something about my day. But then I remember he's no longer a part of me, and I put the phone back down. We can't even go back to being just friends. I did this, and there's no taking it back.

As much as we teased about it, I guess I didn't realize until it was too late that he really had become my best friend. The person I could laugh with and talk to. The person I could be comfortable with. The person I could maybe someday *love*.

Quitting Lucas is one of the hardest things I've ever had to do, but I know one word—one look—from him would weaken my defenses all over again. It's best to go cold turkey, as much as it sucks.

Kelley has also gone into overprotective mode, finding excuses to check-in on me regularly. We've always been close, but it's not unusual for us to go a week or two without seeing each other. Lately, however, I seem to find her at the cottage nearly every day. I like to pretend I'm holding it together pretty well, but she isn't buying it.

Today she brought me lunch, saying she just so happened to be in the area. *Riight.*

"Come on, eat up, Kins."

I stab at a few pieces of chicken in my salad. "I'm just not that hungry right now." She gives me a stern look, causing me to take a bite. "Happy?" I say with a mouthful of lettuce.

Kelley beams as if she's just won an argument. "Yes, thank you. And just for that, you even get dessert." She whips out a bottle of cotton candy flavored vodka from her purse and pours some into our half-empty glasses of lemonade already sitting on the table.

I'm still not a drinker, but somehow today seems like a good day to give it a try. In my attempt to control my feelings, I ended up even more hurt and alone, so a lot of good that did me. Now I just want to forget the pain.

I down the majority of my cup, and Kelley follows suit.

We sit in silence for a minute, each continuing to chew on our own meals . . . and thoughts.

Finally, Kelley speaks up. "Are you ready to tell me what

happened?"

I think about that for a second. Part of me could really use a chance to get it all out in the open, but there's another part of me that is embarrassed by how I acted.

"I just couldn't handle it, Kells. It wasn't going to work out. I'm meant to be alone."

She looks toward the ceiling, as if thinking really hard about something. "I'm not going to lie, you are good on your own. Most people would completely fall apart after everything you've been through, but somehow you seemed to take it as a challenge to find your own way. I mean look at you—living the dream, owning your own business, being your own boss. You risked a lot to do it, but it all ended up working out. And you genuinely love what you do."

She's really good at this whole pep talk thing.

Yeah, who needs Lucas when I have myself?

"But . . ." Kelley adds.

Crap. My smile fades.

"But despite all of that, did you really not notice how much more fulfilling it all was when you had someone to share it with? That you were brighter, happier around Lucas?"

I contemplate that for a minute, not yet willing to confirm nor deny.

"Look, if he did something to hurt you, I'll be the first one to kick him in the nuts, but something tells me this has less to do with him and more to do with your own insecurities. I'd hate to see you lose out on something even greater because you're too scared to give it a chance. You were willing to risk your money and your livelihood for this business, so why not also risk your heart for a chance at love?"

Ugh. I hate it when she sounds like a fortune cookie.

And when she's right.

I was perfectly content to live with my self-inflicted misery, but now that it's been said out loud I can't hide. I was so sure that I would ultimately get hurt that I caused it to happen. Once again, I got in my own way and I'm afraid it's too late to make it right.

"Leave it to the hopeless romantic to be the voice of reason."

"Just call me Jiminy friggin Cricket!"

We both dissolve into a fit of drunken giggles. I can't help but find it amusing that Kelley Brooks, the girl who believes in Prince Charming and happy endings, is also such a realist. She always calls it like it is. Between her and Lucas, I have my own personal bullshit detectors.

Except Lucas is no longer mine, personal or otherwise.

That thought sobers me right up. I let my head fall to the table, covering it with my arms.

"What am I going to do, Kell? Lucas deserves more than a broken girl who can't get out of her own head. He deserves to be happy."

Kelley gently grabs my wrist to pull my arm away from my face. "So do you, Kinsley. And if I had to bet, I think you make him happier than you give yourself credit for. I see the way he looks at you—like you're the only girl in the universe. He's crazy for you, and you're crazy for him. Now you both just need to suck it up so you can go be crazy together."

A LITTLE WHILE AFTER KELLEY leaves, a knock at the front door startles me and I move slowly to see who it is. I'm surprised to see Ryan standing in the doorway, looking disheveled with his shirt crumpled and untucked with his tie loosened.

"Ryan? Is something wrong?" I've never seen him look so unnerved.

"Kins, it's Lucas. Eli had a heart attack and is in the hospital and I haven't seen Lucas this wrecked since . . . well, since his mom got sick. I don't have the first clue as to what happened between you guys, but I know he needs you—even if he's too stubborn to admit it."

As I try to breathe and focus on what Ryan has said. Only a few key words seem to travel all the way to my brain.

Eli . . . hospital . . . Lucas . . . needs you.

Flashes of Lucas lighting up as he talks about his dad collide with images of him looking both sad and broken as he recalls memories of his mother. My mind starts to race as I can think of but one thing: being there for my friend when he needs me most. I remember what it was like to sit all alone in a cold and sterile hospital room, waiting for answers and hoping beyond measure that the doctor with the defeated, tired face isn't coming toward you to gently break some bad news. The thought of ever having to go back to a place like that usually freezes me in some sort of panic, but suddenly my fear is outweighed by my need to see Lucas, to make sure he is OK.

I focus my eyes back on Ryan. "Please, take me to him."

WHEN WE ARRIVE AT THE hospital I let Ryan lead me through the maze of hallways and elevators until we reach a nurse's station on the fifth floor of the west wing. After speaking with the young, pretty nurse in a hushed tone for a moment, she motions for us to wait in the adjoining seating area. Just as I turn to make my way to one of the chairs, I lock eyes with a tired looking Lucas coming down the hall. He freezes a few steps from me, seemingly too shocked to say anything. I, myself, am speechless so we just stand there staring.

Ryan glances between the two of us before announcing,

"I'm going to grab a cup of coffee." He steps away to head back toward the elevators.

I watch Ryan leave and fidget with my hands.

Finally, Lucas breaks the awkward silence. "What are you doing here?"

Wow—that stings. But OK, I guess I deserve it.

"Ryan told me about your dad. How is he?"

"He's stable. They say it was a minor heart attack. They're letting him rest before they run a few more tests, but they say he should be fine."

"I'm glad to hear he'll be OK." I chance a closer look at Lucas' face, noting how exhausted he looks. "And how are you?"

He doesn't answer for a beat, but just as he's about to say something the same nurse from earlier comes over to squeeze his arm.

"Your dad is awake now, Lucas."

His eyes never break from mine and he barely acknowledges the nurse. Again, just when I think he's going to say something, the impatient nurse taps his shoulder to direct him back down the hallway. He gives me a sideways smile and a shrug as he lets the nurse lead him to Eli's room.

I debate waiting in the small seating area for a while, just in case he needs me, but as I turn to sit I see Chelsea heading my way.

"Oh, Kinsley, how is he? Erik told me what happened so I rushed right over. Thanks for being here in the meantime, though." She gives me a hug—actually hugs *me*, the girl who is finally ready to accept that she's in love with a boy she no longer has any claim to. Because that's what I feel for him, isn't it? Deep down, gut-wrenching, crazy, messed up, scary, amazing, beautiful *love*.

But it's too late, and I suddenly feel very much out of place.

Of course Chelsea would be here . . . of course she *should* be here. I had my chance, but now he's hers. And I practically served him up on a silver platter.

I mumble something about having to go and get out of there as quickly as I can.

CHAPTER

twenty-six

Lucas

IT'S ALMOST TOO MUCH TO see Kinsley standing here in the middle of the hospital waiting room, looking so genuinely worried and concerned. At first I think I'm hallucinating.

But it's really her, and I am so overwhelmed with equal parts of regret and relief that I don't know how to react. The past few hours have been an emotional monsoon. Seeing my dad loaded into an ambulance was one of my biggest fears come to life, and all I can remember thinking is *I wish Kinsley was here to help me through this. If I just have her, I can face anything.*

Then seeing her here . . . it was like a nightmare turned into a dream and I can't tell if I'm waking up or falling apart. Then the next thing I know I'm being led by a nurse back down the hospital hallway and my head is still spinning.

As I round the corner into my dad's room, I'm in awe of how big and strong he looks, even lying in a hospital bed after a heart attack. After everything with my mom, he always remained so steady, stepping up to take care of me alone. I've always depended on him to bail me out and offer advice, but perhaps I should have been a little less selfish and should have helped him more in return. Despite his outward composure, I could always tell there was a light in him that permanently dimmed when we lost her, and I've never felt more resolved than now to let him know I've finally grown up. It's my turn to take care of him.

"Hey, Pop. How are you feeling?" I step closer to the side of the bed, lightly clasping his shoulder.

"I'm fine. Must have pushed myself a little too hard on my run this morning. Don't you worry." He pats my hand, ever the reassuring father, putting my fears to rest first.

"Well, I'm going to make sure you have the best doctors and tests to make sure everything is fine. You need to start taking it easy so I'll take over the house chores and help manage your properties."

"I appreciate that, son, but I'm more worried about you taking care of Kinsley. Have you told her what an ass you've been yet?"

Leave it to him to bring this up now. "I've been a little busy riding in ambulances and threatening doctors to make sure you're taken care of. She came to see how you are, though."

"She still here?"

"I'm not sure."

"What are you waiting for? You better go find out." He nods toward the door but I don't move, taking in the beeping machines and wires he's still connected to.

As if sensing my hesitation, he softens his eyes and grabs my arm. "I'm fine now, Lucas. Really. Thank you for being here for me, but now it's time for you to do the same for her."

I reach down to give him a hug, careful not to disturb any of his IVs or wires. I pull back and he squeezes my hand.

He looks at me and smiles before saying, "Go get your girl, Luc. Your mother and I both want nothing more than for you to be happy, and Kinsley's it. Don't let her go."

I smile and squeeze his hand back before turning to do exactly what he says.

I QUICKLY MAKE MY WAY back to the waiting room and scan the chairs filled with anxious, tired bodies for the only brown haired, blue eyed girl I can focus on. As I turn to ask the nurses if they've seen her, I bump into Ryan.

"Hey, man. How's Eli?"

"He's good—he'll be fine. Where's Kinsley?"

"She just took a cab home. I tried to tell her I'd take her, but she was insistent that I stay here with you and Chelsea."

"Chelsea? What's she doing here?"

He shrugs. "I dunno, man, but I think it's time to settle it once and for all."

I nod, knowing exactly what he means. Just then I see Chelsea making her way over with two cups of coffee.

She looks relieved to see me. "Lucas, how's your dad? I came as soon as I heard."

"He's good, Chels. He'll be fine. But listen, we need to talk."

I lead Chelsea down a quieter corridor, out into a small courtyard outside. We sit down on one of the wooden benches.

I look down at my shoes, not sure where to start. I force myself to look into her eyes—it's really not her fault, and I'm the one who has to be a man and own up to my mistakes.

"Chelsea, I want you to know that there was a time I thought I loved you. I know when I broke things off, I made it seem like I might be able to change, so you stuck around in the hopes I would get my shit together." She looks at me eagerly. I know this next part is going to hurt the most, but she needs to know the truth.

"And recently I did change. I discovered that it's not that I'm incapable of love . . . I just had to find the right person." I look at her gently, trying to convey my sincere apology.

The defeat shows plainly on her face as she realizes I'm not talking about her. "It's Kinsley, isn't it?" she whispers.

I nod. "I'm sorry Chelsea. You deserve way better than how I treated you. I should have let you go a long time ago rather than allow you to hold out hope for us. I'm an asshole for that, and I'm sorry. Just know that I don't regret our time together. Without you I never would have been able to truly find out who I am, and for that you will always be special."

I squeeze her hand, hoping I'm making sense.

She gives my hand a gentle squeeze back and lets out a long exhale. "You know, Luc, I always knew I wasn't the one for you. Deep down, anyway, even if I didn't want to admit it. Yes, there was a part of me that thought you were just a little lost and only needed some time to find your way back to me, but the more I saw you change these past few weeks—and knew it had every-thing to do with her—I realized she's the one you were looking for, not me. I let you hold on, so it's as much my fault as it is yours."

She leans over to give me a hug, one that I know will be our last. She stands and makes her way to the door before stop-ping and turning to look at me one last time. "She loves you, you know. Even if she's not ready to say it, I can tell she does."

With that she heads back inside, and for the first time I feel a genuine emotion when it comes to Chelsea. *Closure.*

I make my own way back inside and catch Ryan walking down the hall. I'm already halfway to the staircase when I call back, "Hey Ry. Stay here with my dad. I'll be back."

I sprint down the five flights of stairs and hail my own cab to head straight to the cottage. I just hope I'm not too late.

CHAPTER

twenty-seven

Kinsley

WHAT WAS I THINKING GOING to see Lucas? Just as I expected, the moment I saw him my heart instantly fluttered back to life. I was supposed to be there for him, for Eli, yet I could barely muster up the courage to ask how they were doing. After seeing Chelsea, I knew I couldn't stay, so I ran away from my feelings yet again.

The rain starts to pour just as I get out of the cab. How fitting.

I plop down on the couch in the front sitting area and stare out at the raindrops pelting the window when I'm suddenly startled by a loud knock at the door. I cautiously make my way to the entryway, hoping it's not more bad news. When I pull the door open and see Lucas standing on the porch, completely soaked, staring at me with his fierce hazel eyes, I'm overcome with so much emotion of what I feel for him and all the things I should have said and done the past few weeks that I can't help but throw myself into his arms. The fact that I feel him grab on and hold me tight is all it takes for me to burst into tears.

AFTER WHAT FEELS LIKE HOURS of Lucas just holding me on the cold, wet porch, he gently pulls me inside the cottage. He leads me to the couch and startles me when he commands, "Take off your clothes."

I must be in shock or something, because I do so without hesitation. I have a feeling this man could ask me to commit a capital crime right now and I'd do it without question.

As I shimmy out of my wet clothes so I'm standing in nothing by my underthings, Lucas grabs a towel from the bathroom and wraps it around me, rubbing my shoulders to generate heat.

"Funny, this is sort of how we first met." The sparkle in his eyes makes me want to cry all over again. "I guess the movies aren't as far from real life as I thought, either." He looks down at his own wet clothes and gives a shy, sideways smile.

I don't deserve his kindness right now. I thank my lucky stars I seem to have a second chance, and I'll be damned if I don't tell him how I really feel. I'm done running away.

"I'm so sorry, Lucas. I'm sorry I pushed you away . . . I thought it was better to end things before either of us got really hurt, and it turns out that's exactly what happened because of me . . . I get it if you can't forgive me, but I just want to be honest . . . I know you're with Chelsea now, and I want you to be happy, but I didn't realize I'd lose my best friend in the process, and I . . . I miss you."

There goes that word vomit again. But at least it's the truth, even if it does come out as a run-on, jumbled mess of thoughts. I bite my lip as Lucas stills his hands on my shoulders.

"I miss you so fucking much, Kins. And I'm the one who should be apologizing. I'm not going to be with Chelsea or anyone else, now or ever. You're the one for me. Since the moment I first saw you at that wedding, it's only been you. I was just so hurt that you were pulling away that I let my stupid ass pride get in the way. I once told you that you could always count on me to call you on your shit, so I shouldn't have let you walk away—I should have proved to you that you can always trust me to be there for you."

I'm warmed (and relieved) by his words, but I look up at him confused by his confession about noticing me prior to our meeting at the cottage. Something about hearing that makes my heart beat even faster. "Wedding?" *No, it couldn't be . . .*"The one at Woodwind Hills?"

He nods. "Something about you nearly knocked me on my ass. I couldn't stop thinking about the cute mystery woman in the dirty t-shirt." He chuckles, teasing me.

I'm stunned. I never really gave things like fate or destiny much merit, but I seem to have been misguided about a lot of things. "I guess I should confess that I noticed you, then, too." I blush at the admission.

"Really?" He looks just as shocked, but quickly recovers. "And what was it that you noticed, exactly?" He tilts his head playfully.

"Honestly?" I rake my eyes over his body. "Your ass." That makes us both laugh. "Well, before that, it was something about the way you smiled. I remember thinking that girl you were with was lucky to be able to make you so happy."

He caresses my arms. "You, Kinsley Moore, make me insanely fucking happy." His arms still again. "I'm sorry I didn't let you know that."

I shake my head before averting my eyes to stare at little bits of lint clinging to the towel draped around me. "It's not your fault. I just don't have the best record when it comes to trusting people, and then everything happened with Chelsea so I freaked out. But you're not like them. I know that."

"Like who?" He says it softly and gently, as if afraid I'm going to push him away again.

Not this time.

I look up into his soft, understanding eyes before finally admitting, "My father . . . my ex boyfriend. All the guys I've trusted before." I take a deep breath and relax my shoulders before deciding to start at the beginning.

"I always thought I had a great childhood, you know? My parents and I lived in a nice house, I had lots of friends, we went on vacations, and it was generally pretty normal. I didn't have a lot of extended family, so it was really just the three of us. When I was in elementary school and started making friends, I became old enough to realize my parents weren't actually married. When I asked my dad why, he brushed it off and said it was only because he was waiting to throw my mom the biggest wedding she could ever dream of. Since they seemed happy enough, I didn't think it was a big deal."

"Then one day when I was in middle school I found a napkin with a phone number and a lipstick print in my dad's coat pocket. He dismissed it and reassured me he loved me and my mom and it was nothing. There were other small things over the years—strange phone calls, extended business trips—but my dad continued to act like the perfect guy. When he was around, that is. My mom brushed off his long absences by telling me he had to work, but something felt off about it."

I pause for a second to collect my thoughts, and Lucas rubs my arm in the sweetest, most encouraging way. I've never told this entire story with every single, painful detail to anyone before—not even Kelley. She just knows the general gist of what happened. But I know telling Lucas every last part will somehow free me from having to feel so alone.

"Then when I was seventeen I found a stash of letters and pictures hidden in the closet at our vacation home near the beach. We used to spend some summer weekends there, but otherwise it stayed empty most of the time. Or I thought it did . . . at this point I put it all together and knew that my dad had been seeing other women my entire life. When I confronted him he could barely look at me, but still tried making up weak excuses. My mom even defended him, but I could tell from the look in her eyes she was hurt. Whether she knew and chose to ignore it or she really had no idea, I'll never know, but once I brought it all out in the open there was no going back. I kept thinking back to how great our life seemed, but then felt like it was all just a lie and I couldn't trust either of them to commit to me or us as a real family and tell me the truth. He moved out a week later, and I barely spoke to him after that. I was almost eighteen, so as soon as I could I went out on my own and didn't really keep in touch with either of them. I knew my mom still saw him occasionally, which I could never understand and we often fought about. She would just say it was complicated. About five years ago they were driving together, and a truck ran a light and hit them head on."

I will the tears stinging the backs of my eyes to stay there, but one slips through and rolls slowly down my cheek. Lucas wipes the droplet from my face with his thumb. "It's not your fault, Kins. You know that. It's a fucked up situation, but to me it still sounds like they both just wanted you to be happy."

Hearing his reassuring words is comforting, but I know I have to finish.

"At the time I was still dating this guy I met shortly after I moved out. Looking back he was kind of a jerk, but I was desperate for attention I guess. I wanted to feel connected. I really thought he could be the one to save me, and when he told me he would take care of me, I trusted him. He knew I didn't have anyone else and made me believe we could have a life together. When my parents died, shortly after the funeral I found out he had been cheating on me pretty much the whole time we were together. It was as if the blows just kept on coming, and at this point I was numb to almost any emotion. I just remember this feeling of extreme emptiness. I wasn't even upset when he finally broke up with me. I just didn't understand why I never seemed to be enough for anyone. After that I made a decision to never get too close. A few times I tried being with other guys, thinking maybe I would feel something again, but I never fully trusted anyone enough to let go. I learned to be confident and detached, which is what I thought they wanted, but eventually they would leave and I would be left on my own again. It just became easier to accept that to be my life. I just felt so helpless and out of control, from that point on I knew it was easier to be closed off . . . to be in control and protect myself. I even tried to shut Kelley out for a while, but thankfully she didn't give up and is the only one who kept me somewhat sane."

I can feel Lucas tense up, from his jaw right down to his fist, so I gently squeeze his hand to let him know I'm OK—that it's helping me to get it all out in the open.

"Despite how messed up everything got, I miss both my parents more than anything and wish it could have been different. I felt so betrayed and then they were gone and it's just been easier to push people away. To be independent and rely only on myself. To never let anyone get too close. But you make me feel different. You really seem to see me and I've felt safe with you from the moment I met you. You changed me, Luc, and you make me want something I never thought I would again."

He angles his head at me questioningly before whispering in a slightly gravelly, choked up voice, "What's that?"

"A family."

I can't help but smile as I think about all the things Lucas makes me want and feel. I can see a future with him, and while it scares me, I find myself more excited than afraid.

Luc stares at me intently for a minute as if contemplating something before getting an all too serious look on his face. "You know what I think?"

I swallow nervously. This is it . . . he might change his mind now that he knows how messed up my life has been. I can only look at him with hopeful, expectant eyes.

He leans in close before whispering, "I think we would make some really cute babies together." His playful smile is just what we need to break the emotional tension. The fact that he can always tell when my thoughts become too heavy, too much for me, makes my heart melt. I never thought I would find someone who could read me so completely, and I'm so relieved that we can go back to our playful nature I can't help but laugh.

I tease him back, "Maybe someday we'll find out, but for now we should probably just practice making them . . . practice makes perfect, right?"

I must catch him off guard again, because he lightly chuckles, "You're crazy. In the best way, that is."

"And you love it,' I reply as an automatic reflex.

He stops laughing and looks at me with his soft, serious eyes again. "I love *you*."

I didn't think it was possible, but my smile and heart grow even bigger. Without hesitation, I easily reply, "I love you too, Lucas. More than you'll ever know."

CHAPTER

twenty-eight

Lucas

FINALLY ADMITTING TO KINSLEY THAT I love her—and hearing her say it back—has got to be my new favorite thing. Followed closely by both making her laugh and watching her come, that is.

I kiss her greedily, although I try to be gentle as I realize the weight of everything she just admitted to me about her past. I know there was no way I could have possibly known just how fragile her trust issues are, but I still feel like an ass for giving her the slightest notion that I could ever be like her father or her as-shat of an ex-boyfriend. I already abandoned her once, and that is one time too many. Time to step up and prove the way I feel about her.

The way she lets out a breathless, soft moan at the base of her throat and grinds closer to me in nothing but a towel has my dick already gearing up. I slowly slide the towel down her shoulders, taking a good look as she stands before me.

It's the most beautiful I've ever seen her: no makeup, no fancy clothes, her hair tangled and damp.

Just her, natural and perfect, and she's all mine. For good this time.

I remove my own soaked clothes, then I start to kiss across her neck. I know she likes that. She tangles her hands in my hair and holds me close to her chest. I help her remove the rest of what little clothing she has left on, and soon we are both naked and ready.

I grab her waist and help her down on the couch behind us. She lies back and I hoist myself up to position myself gently on top of her. I stroke her face, lost in the emotion showing in her eyes, yet neither of us say anything. We don't have to—we can both feel it.

I kiss her lips again before slowly pushing myself inside her, savoring the way we fit together like two interlocking puzzle pieces. Her eyes never stray from mine as we move together in a slow and passionate pace. If I thought sex with Kinsley was amazing, making love to her is beyond any sort of words or description.

But then again, I think we've always been this way together, even if we didn't want to admit it.

She grabs onto my ass, pulling me closer and deeper and I can tell she's getting close. I lean down, tucking my head close to her neck and whisper, "I love you," just before she says the same and we both explode in unison.

I cup her face with both hands and kiss her forehead before looking deep into her blue eyes. "I promise I will always be there for you, Kins. You can trust me with your whole heart and I will do everything in my power not to break it. I am human, however, so please understand if I still act like a douchebag sometimes.

But I promise it will never be to intentionally hurt you."

I sit up and tuck her hair behind her ear. She grabs onto my arm before saying, "I know that, Luc. And I can't be perfect, either, but know that I'm trying. Deep down I know I can trust you, but that doesn't mean I'll never have doubts. I just want to be enough for you."

The fact that she could ever think she isn't enough shatters me. Now I know it's her past that made her feel this way, but if it takes the rest of my goddamn life I will make sure she feels loved and cherished.

I hug her close to me. "You are more than enough, babe. You're everything."

I give her a quick kiss on the cheek and push myself up from the couch. I wrap her back in the towel and pull on my own jeans. I give her another long, lingering kiss on her soft lips before adding, "And I plan to spend the rest of my life proving it to you." Then I turn to leave while sporting a charming, mischievous grin.

I've got some planning to do.

~epilogue~

Kinsley

THE DAY AFTER LUCAS AND I finally admitted all of our feelings, pasts, and fears, I woke up at the cottage to find dozens of ranunculuses scattered about the front lawn. From my loft window I could see they made out the shape of a heart with "L+K" spelled out in the center. Taped to the window was a note that read:

This is just the beginning. xx L

And for the next few weeks Lucas continued to shower me with surprises and remained extremely attentive and loyal. I tried telling him that it wasn't necessary—that all I need is him—but, just like me, he can be pretty stubborn.

What warms my heart even more is the fact that he doesn't even do anything particularly grand or extravagant. It's not that he's trying to buy my affection or trust, he's genuinely showing how he feels.

Eli was released from the hospital with a clean bill of health, and the following Friday Lucas brought us both to *Pedro's*. We shared a delicious meal while joking and telling stories. At the end of the night Eli hugged me goodbye and whispered that he was proud of me. Lucas didn't have to say it, but I knew this was his way of showing me I was part of their tradition—and part of their family—now. The three of us continue to go there every single week, although we usually see each other more often than that.

A few days after that Lucas brought me to the cemetery to introduce me to his mom. He told her that she would have liked me and that I'm beautiful and smart. We left a special vase of flowers I arranged just for her.

A week later Lucas asked me to move in with him, telling me that he wanted us to have a home together . . . except the deal was he actually wanted to move into the cottage. I cried happy tears and we christened just about every surface in my—*our*—house that night in celebration.

The day after that he came home with another tattoo—a small, delicate heart on the inside of his left ring finger. He simply shrugged and told me it was so I would always know my heart was in his hands.

Like any strong couple we still have our arguments or disagreements, but we made a pact to never go to bed angry.

OK, and I'll even admit that sometimes I maybe pick a fight just so we can make up.

What? Lucas is very . . . ahem . . . *thorough* . . . when it comes to being sure we've made up.

IT'S BEEN TWO MONTHS OF us navigating our new life together, and while for the most part it's been great, today has just been one of those craptastic days. A bride completely changed her color palette at the last minute, I accidentally broke three vases, and a shipment I was expecting came in all wrong.

By the time I drag myself out of the workroom, I'm less than pleasant, despite seeing that Lucas has made me a candlelit dinner. I barely give him a kiss on the cheek or acknowledge the meal before gluing myself to my phone to sort out the messed up order.

"Hey babe, you care to join me for this lovely meal?" Lucas gestures to the spread before him on the table.

"Maybe later. I've got to get this order straightened out."

Lucas gets up from the table to stand in front of me, sliding my phone from my hand. "How about we eat first, and then you can get back to being a workaholic."

Well that was the wrong thing to say given the current mood I'm in. "Workaholic? Well excuse me for taking my job so seriously. It's only how I make my living, no big deal or anything."

I snatch my phone back from his hand and go to storm to the bedroom. Lucas grabs my arm and pulls me back to him before I get very far. "You know I didn't mean it like that, Kins. I just thought tonight could be special."

Tired and frustrated, the words are out of my mouth before I can stop them. "And what's so special about tonight that it can't wait?"

Lucas lets go of my arm and reaches into his pocket. He pulls out a small, black box before opening it to reveal a beautiful, simple diamond ring. I am rendered shocked and speechless as a playful smile lights up his face and he places it on the counter.

He puts one hand on either side of my face, making sure I have his full attention before politely asking, "Will you fucking marry me?"

And just like that everything else melts away as my own smile breaks free. I leap into Lucas's arms, causing us both to tumble back as I attack him with kisses and mumble a "Hell yes" against his perfect lips.

The End.

acknowledgements

TO THE BESTEST HUSBAND A girl can ask for—Clifford, thank you for being the one person I can count on for anything and everything. I love you af&1d. And then some.

To my mom, brother, and the rest of my family—Hopefully you can look past some of the dirty words here and be proud I took a chance writing something fun. I know you support me in everything I do, and that means the world to me. (And at least I'm putting my English degree to use!)

To Ashley W., Jennifer C., Hazel R., and Ellie—Thank you for being such sweet beta readers! It was scary letting complete strangers read my first drafts, but your thoughts, comments, and ideas were invaluable.

To Kari March—Thanks for the beautiful cover design!

To Danielle and Shannon at DVE—I seriously can't express how much all of your editorial insight was a help to me, both for the development of this book and as a growing author in general. You made my leap into publishing a little less scary, and for that I will forever be grateful.

To Christine and Nichole at Perfectly Publishable—Thank you for polishing this baby up and getting it ready for the world!

And finally, to anybody who reads this—The fact you did makes my heart do a little happy dance.

about the author

WHEN SHE'S NOT MAKING CONFETTI as head honcho over at The Confetti Bar (*theconfettibar.com*), co-dreaming with creative women through Monarch Workshop (*monarchworkshop.com*), and blogging about her health & wellness journey going sugar-free at Simple Unsweet (*simpleunsweet.com*), Jessica loves to spend her nights getting caught up in imaginary worlds.

She lives in central CT with her husband, Clifford, and the cutest cat EVER, named Curious.

She loves colorful things, making people smile, things that smell good, and is obsessed with lemon water. And glitter. Lots of glitter.

She also loves, well . . . love. (She's a sucker for a sweet story.)

You can check out what she's up to at *jshbooks.com* and on Instagram (@jshbooks)

Want to know anything else? Feel free to say hi at *lovejshbooks@gmail.com!*

www.ingramcontent.com/pod-product-compliance
Lightning Source LLC
Chambersburg PA
CBHW032128170626
46808CB00006B/2145